Belonging

JAMES H LEWIS

JAMES H LEWIS

Contents

One

AT THE BEGINNING of the day, Sarah Mathews was confident in her identity as a wife, mother, daughter, and entrepreneur. Hours later, she was no longer certain who she was.

The morning began innocently, Sarah striking a casual but confident pose as she stared into a camera lens. She smiled, her mouth slightly open but not enough to reveal her dazzling white teeth. A rectangular soft light filled her field of view. Behind her, a scrim-mounted backlight illuminated the reddish highlights in her brown hair while three spots lit the background.

"You may have heard 'experts' say you can't make a decent loaf of sourdough using a bread machine," she said. "I'm Sourdough Sal, and today I'll prove them wrong." She ended with a broader smile.

"Perfect," said a voice beyond the lights. "Do you need to stop for a moment?"

"Let's go on." Sarah paused before speaking. Cheryl Price, her creative director and the voice behind the camera, would replace the fifteen-second gap with the opening billboard and theme of her weekly program.

"I like to get my hands into the dough, even as I'm mixing it," Sarah said. "But you may have so many things to do, you don't have the time. Jeanine of Winnipeg, Manitoba, asked how she could use her bread machine to make sourdough white. I'm glad to share a technique I've developed."

During the first episodes in the series, she'd invented the names of those requesting recipes to suggest the entire nation was watching. She no longer needed to fake it; with more than a dozen lessons online and a growing audience, new requests arrived daily, overwhelming her inbox.

Removing the bowl of her bread machine—careful to mention the brand name BreadSense—Sarah placed it on the Elettrica Cuccina electronic scale and measured first water and then sourdough starter. Cheryl switched to a ceiling-mounted camera pointing downward at the work surface to capture the step.

Mentioning the brand name of the bread flour, Sarah said, "Always measure ingredients by weight, because the volume of flour varies with its moisture content."

Sarah had been marketing director for a chain of health clubs and had been on pregnancy leave when the COVID pandemic hit. After her son Kellan was born, the company had closed its doors. Cheryl, an art director for their advertising agency, was collateral damage, let go when her agency lost three valuable contracts. While Sarah was financially secure, she needed a creative outlet, and Cheryl needed income. Thus was their Sourdough Sal partnership formed.

After placing the ingredients in the bread machine, Sarah turned it on. A series of loud thumps filled the studio Victor, her husband, had built at one end of their basement. As the machine's paddle churned the flour and water, Penny, Cheryl's teenage daughter, moved an iPhone closer to record the process. Cheryl would later edit this clip into the finished video and dissolve into the next scene.

"Mommy! Mommy!" Sarah looked down to see her twenty-one-month-old son had wandered onto the set, followed by Vivian, the college student who sometimes looked after him. Sarah picked the child up without missing a beat and sat him on the edge of the counter. "Mommy's making bread, Kellan. Do you want to taste it after I've finished?"

The child laughed and nodded his head. "Let me put you down for your nap while I finish showing these nice people how to bake it."

She picked him up, handing him to Vivian. "Sorry about that, Mrs. M," the girl said. "He just scooted away and was down the stairs before I could stop him."

Because you were listening to music on your phone, Sarah thought. Cheryl would edit the scene, "fix it in post," to use her expression.

"Being a mom means learning to be flexible," she said. "That's what this lesson is about: learning how to do traditional things in new ways."

Cheryl stopped recording, and Sarah replaced the bread machine with an identical model. After peering inside to make certain the dough had risen, she nodded to Cheryl to resume the recording.

"Four hours have passed," she said, "and look at the beautiful dough we've produced." She lifted the white blob out of the machine's bowl without deflating it, pulled out the paddle, and began shaping it into a ball as she spoke. "Let's spray our plastic rising container and lay the dough in it, seam side up," she said, going through the motions as she spoke. "I'll cover it with the lid and place it in the refrigerator to proof overnight."

Production halted as Sarah changed her blouse and apron. She removed the container from the refrigerator and replaced it with an identical container from off camera. "The starter has had overnight to work its magic," she said. "I removed it from the refrigerator two hours ago to let it come up to room temperature. I've preheated my oven to 475 degrees with my Ardmore Dutch oven inside."

Using two ovenproof gloves—OvenSafe by name—she took the pot out of the oven, removed the risen dough from the plastic container, and lowered it gingerly into the Dutch oven. She scored the top, brushed it with an egg mixture, and sprinkled sesame seeds over it. She returned the pot to the range and, with an exaggerated motion, lowered the temperature to 425 degrees. She did this for show, as this oven wasn't hooked up.

"Twenty minutes have passed, and I'm going to lift the lid and finish our loaf uncovered." She did so as she spoke, not allowing the camera to see the loaf, which was unchanged.

Another three minutes passed while Sarah prepared for the last scene. She swapped the cold pot with an identical one from a hot oven out of camera range.

"It's been forty minutes since the loaf went in, and I think," she said as she opened the door to the prop oven, "it's ready." Donning the other mitt, she removed the blazing hot container, tilted it toward the camera, and upended the bread onto a metal rack. She waited a moment while Penny moved her iPhone in on the steaming loaf.

When Cheryl gave the all-clear, Sarah moved the hot loaf out of sight and replaced it with another. "After an hour, our loaf has cooled enough to slice it." She cut off the heel and two slices, holding one up to her head and burying her face in it. Emitting a long sigh, she said, "I made this beautiful, fragrant loaf of sourdough bread with the help of the BreadSense machine. And they said it can't be done."

Sarah slathered butter over the other slice and took a bite. "In our next episode, I'll show you how to make whole wheat bread using the same technique. If you enjoyed this lesson, please subscribe, leave a comment below, and share the link with your friends. And if you'd like to purchase your own BreadSense machine at a substantial discount, click the link below this lesson. I'm Sourdough Sal. Here's to more baking in the wild."

She smiled at the camera and held the pose until Cheryl called, "Cut!" Another episode of Sourdough Sal was in the can.

As Cheryl packed away their gear, Sarah sat on a barstool at the counter of her kitchen studio, hunched over her notebook computer. She rested her left foot on the bottom rung of the chair while extending her right behind her. "Ouch," she said as her son slammed his bumper car into her leg. "Mommy's working, Kellan."

"Toast, Mommy. Want toast."

She rose, cut a slice of bread from the finished loaf, and shoved it into the toaster oven. "Do you want butter or peanut butter?"

Kellan pointed at the tray containing the yellow stick. "Can you say butter, honey?"

He let out an unintelligible burble. Sarah sighed, lathered the toast, and cut it into four sections before putting it on his tray. As she returned to work, Kellan careened to the opposite end of the basement, set up as his playroom.

She had already responded to the latest notes on her YouTube channel. She now turned to her email, beginning with the sourdoughsal account. "LUV your informative videos," MollyS wrote from Peoria. "How did you get started?"

Sarah inserted a few lines of stock copy from a program Cheryl had written for her and dispatched her reply over an

HTML signature containing links to her channel, Facebook page, Instagram feed, and Twitter handle. She dispatched the subsequent five messages just as quickly. Cheryl's program had once allowed her to provide "personal" answers to seventeen emails in an hour, a record that still stood.

Kellan cried out, having wedged his bumper car between two overstuffed chairs. "Damn it, Victor," she said to her absent husband, "I've asked you not to move them."

"Dammit," Kellan said.

"'Darn it,' Kellan. That's what Mommy said. 'Darn it.'"

"Dammit," he repeated and erupted in a chortle that shook his entire body.

She laughed along with him. Few things gave her more joy than listening whenever he cracked himself up. "And time to change the royal diaper from the smell of things." She performed his ablutions and placed him on the floor with an empty pot, wooden ladle, and ring of measuring spoons.

Her marketing duties completed for the day, she turned to her personal email. "How did I get on so many lists?" she said, as her stubby fingers highlighted a long row of messages and deleted them. She read one or two, answered none, and came to one from Ancestry. "Eleanor Frangos has sent you a message."

She was tempted to ignore it. Mapping her family tree had been Victor's idea, not hers, and she had found time to enter only the two generations she knew about. Her DNA test had been a fiasco, and she had never heard of Eleanor Frangos. Nevertheless, her curiosity got the better of her.

> I am exploring my family history and have come across your name. Your DNA test shows we are cousins, and I am trying to determine how we are connected. My mother, Sophia, has a sister, Petra, who has a daughter and a son. Her brother, Theo, died in his late teens in an automobile acci-

dent. He never married. Still, I wonder if he might have fathered a child and never told us about it. Are you his daughter?

I'm sorry to bother you, but there must be a connection. Can you help me? You can respond here or write to me ...

And here she shared her email address and phone number. Sarah recognized the 304 area code as coming from West Virginia. She thought for a moment, her right heel beating a nervous rhythm on the floor, then wrote a response.

I regret to tell you we are not related. Unfortunately, Ancestry has made a mistake, perhaps mixing up my DNA test with someone else's.

My parents are Steven and Lillian Lindstrom. They had me late in life. My mother called me her miracle baby until I asked her to stop. We live in Upper St. Clair, a suburb of Pittsburgh, and have since I was three....

Sarah paused and reread what she'd written. A chill came over her as she reviewed the line she had not finished. She deleted the second paragraph. *Oversharing*, she told herself. "I wish you good fortune in researching your heritage," she wrote and hit the send button.

"Damned fools." She closed her notebook computer. Behind her, Kellan echoed her words.

Victor was chasing Kellan around the family room on his hands and knees when Sarah called them to dinner. Through their dining-room window, snowflakes chased each other in horizontal streaks. "Pork tenderloin in mustard sauce," she announced as she brought their plates to the table.

"My favorite. I married well," he said with a smile.

As she cut small pieces of pork for Kellan and ladled orecchiette onto his tray, her husband asked how her taping had gone, and she inquired into progress on his latest home design. With the preliminaries out of the way, she said, "Not everything went well today."

Victor raised his eyebrows in a question, but before she could continue, Kellan shouted. "Abocabo."

"Say please, Kellen."

"Pweedze." He pounded his little spoon on the tray of his high chair.

She selected a fresh avocado from a basket on the table, cut it open, and spooned the ripe fruit onto his tray. "Who's child is this?" Victor said as Kellan painted his face in the green stuff en route to his mouth.

"Don't worry," she replied with a laugh, "he'll graduate to burgers and franks soon enough."

"You were saying?"

She laid her knife and fork on her plate and brushed aside a dark curl. "A woman sent me a note on Ancestry today claiming I'm her cousin." She summarized the message and said, "It comes from that botched DNA test."

Her father, Steven Lindstrom, came from a long line of Swedish immigrants; his father had dropped the ö in favor of the unadorned o before Steven entered grade school. Her mother, Lillian, was of Scots-Irish heritage with some German lineage thrown in. Sarah's DNA results, however, placed her forebears around the Mediterranean, more than half from Greece. None of the suggested relationships made sense to her, unfamiliar names that lay nowhere on her nascent family tree. She'd taken one look and shelved the results as a mistake.

"Just ignore it," Victor said.

"That's what I'm doing, but this false report is out there for anyone in the world to see."

"Not everyone can see it. Ancestry found a DNA match and notified this woman. They probably notified you as well."

"I've ignored most of their messages," she said, transferring her last bite from plate to mouth. "I don't know what made me open this one."

"If it bothers you that much, redo the test. I'll look into it after Kellan goes night-night."

"I have neither the time nor the interest," she said. "I'm sorry you ever got me into this."

Victor held his tongue, knowing it was perilous to pursue a point on which she'd decided. To change the subject, he said, "I'll clean up."

She was already on her feet, collecting dishes and utensils. "If you'll bathe your son, I'll bathe the dishes."

He tucked his giggling toddler under one arm and trundled him to the guest bathroom, swinging him gently as he went. "Don't make him throw up," she called.

"Mommy says not to throw up," he said as he ran water into the tub until the temperature was right, then slid Kellan's yellow plastic tub beneath the faucet. "You're outgrowing this, little man. Please stop."

"Ducky!"

Holding the toddler's shoulder with one arm, he reached above him for the bath toys. Kellan splashed water over his face, howling with glee. As his son wiggled and thrashed in the water, Victor thought about the dinnertime conversation. As an architect and contractor, he had to be precise, but Sarah went beyond that. She was meticulous. In four years of marriage, he'd learned his pajamas were not to touch the floor but to be placed on the outer hook on the back of their bathroom door. Everything had to be done just so and had to be done now. If something was awry—an item or a plan—she stopped whatever she was doing until she made it right.

He hoped the Ancestry mix-up wouldn't become a big deal.

~

"You may have heard 'experts' say you can't make a decent loaf of sourdough using a bread machine. I'm Sourdough Sal, and today I'll prove them wrong." Sarah's face disappeared from Cheryl's 43-inch computer monitor as the music swelled and a cartoon version of Sarah wielded a rolling pin to paint the words "Sourdough Sal" on the screen.

The pair sat side-by-side at Cheryl's console as the edited version of the previous week's lesson rolled by. Cheryl kept one eye on the screen and the other on her partner, waiting for her inevitable nit-picking. It was not long in coming. "Let me see that again."

Cheryl inched the control bar back twenty seconds and hit play. "Right there," Sarah said. "I wish you'd taken the overhead shot at this point."

"That's how we blocked it, but your hands were in the way. I cut to the shot the moment it was clear."

"All right," she said, but Cheryl could tell she was still dissatisfied.

"This would be easier if I could iso all four cameras and combine them in post, rather than switching the three fixed cameras live."

"We can't afford it right now. We haven't even repaid the equipment loan."

Cheryl sighed and nodded. She had been furloughed just before the Christmas holiday and was living on unemployment while she searched for a job. Sarah's project had given her a shot at independence, but the venture needed to turn a profit soon so she could draw a salary.

"We don't have a shot of the oven thermostat," Sarah said. "I tell them to turn it down to 425, but we don't see me doing it."

"Is it necessary? I can place the instructions on a super at the bottom of the screen."

"That would be great, but seeing it would be even better."

Cheryl closed her eyes and rested her neck against the headrest of her office chair. Would Sarah never be satisfied? "It's just a YouTube video. We're not going after an Emmy here."

"But don't you want it to be right?"

Cheryl rolled her eyes in frustration, then had a thought. "We used that shot in the third episode. I'll grab it and insert it."

"May I see it?"

Cheryl suppressed another sigh and loaded the episode, scrubbing through the control bar until she reached the point where Sarah had turned down the oven's temperature. "I'll lift this clip and lay it into the scene."

"Hmm." Cheryl waited for what would come next. "I'm not wearing the same blouse I did at Thursday's taping, and my wrist is in the frame," Sarah said. "Someone is bound to notice."

"Short of bringing in a camera and recording that one shot—"

"Use the iPhone."

"You'll have to go home and change blouses. What if I insert this shot and put a little box with the correct temperature over your sleeve?"

Cheryl counted the seconds. "I guess that will work."

"I'll make it work."

Sarah didn't respond, and Cheryl accepted her silence as

agreement. Her partner's pickiness made editing a greater burden than it should have been. *On the other hand*, she told herself, *her attention to detail makes the taping a breeze. Half a loaf....*

~

Sarah's bread machine ground to a halt as a burning smell filled the room. She pulled the plug to avoid damaging the motor. *Do I have too much whole wheat flour, too little water, or should I reduce the size of the loaf?* She was to tape this episode in three days and had yet to perfect the recipe. *Why did I tease this lesson without testing it first?*

She opened her computer to study some of her other whole wheat recipes, searching for inspiration. A notification popped up in the corner of her screen, telling her she had a message from Eleanor Frangos. She considered ignoring it, but figuring this might be an apology, opened it.

> Pardon me for writing again, but I want to give you a bit more family history. Our patriarch, the first to emigrate to the US, was Yiannis Panos in 1908. He came from the part of Greece occupied by the Ottoman Empire. When Turkey began drafting Greeks to fight their countrymen, Yiannis joined a group of fellow villagers and came to West Virginia, which was recruiting miners. A year after his arrival, he sent for his wife, Sofia, my great-grandmother, after whom my mother is named.

She rattled on, describing the ensuing generations up to the present moment. Then came the kicker. "I'm telling you this because you are linked to our family somehow. Ancestry says you're a cousin, but perhaps you're a second cousin. So please recheck your family history and determine where you fit in."

What an obstinate, obtuse woman. Sarah began writing a reply, but signed out without posting it. Eleanor Frangos did not merit a response.

Her baby monitor showed Kellan had awakened from his nap. She left the studio kitchen, took the stairs to the main level, entered his bedroom, and scooped him up.

Another dirty diaper. *And Victor wants another child? Not until this one is in his big boy pants.* She brought him into the bathroom, cleaned him up as best she could, and finished by hosing off his bottom in the shower. As she dried him and put on a fresh diaper, she glimpsed herself in the mirror. Old fears and memories flooded back—strange looks from her friends' parents and the inevitable, "Who do you take after?" She examined her brown, curly hair, studied her olive-colored skin, and stared into the reflection of her green eyes.

Could there be some family connection of which she was unaware? She would have to ask her mother. The question was how to pose the question without upsetting her.

Two

"WHAT'S THE OCCASION?" Lilly Lindstrom said as she hung her winter coat in the front closet. "And how's my little lad?"

Kellan raced to embrace his grandmother's left leg, looking up at her with a grin that warmed the room. She reached to pick him up, but he wriggled from her grasp. "He's getting independent, isn't he?"

"Is he ever," Sarah said.

"But why the sudden invitation?" Her blue eyes lit up as a grin spread across her face. "Don't tell me you're—"

"No, Mom, I'm not. You and Victor. Maybe you should have the baby for him."

Her mother sniffed, unwilling to acknowledge any conversation that touched on the subject of s-e-x, no matter how tangential the allusion.

"I thought it would be fun to get together. We haven't talked since—"

"Sunday," Lilly said. "But if that's pea purée I smell, scallops can't be far behind. I welcome the invitation."

Sarah placed Kellan in his high chair and gave him crackers

to snack on while she finished the meal. She removed pear salads from the refrigerator, dressed them with balsamic vinegar and olive oil, and asked Lilly to carry them to the table while she seared the scallops in ghee. A shake of paprika to finish them, and she mounded four scallops on the two beds of the pea, garlic, and cream preparation.

She sliced a scallop and placed it on Kellan's tray. He stared at it for a moment, eyeing it with suspicion. "Abocabo!" he demanded. "Pweedze." She scooped out the green fruit, which he stuffed into his maw with oily fingers.

They spoke of nothing in particular—Victor's latest project, a mini-mansion in neighboring Peters Township, Lilly's service as a deacon in the Presbyterian church, Sarah's YouTube channel, and whether Steven would retire now that he was nearing seventy.

"They'll have to carry him out, dear," Lilly said. She peered over her glasses and said, "Something's on your mind."

Sarah wiped Kellan's hands and sent him to prowl the house, then refilled their wineglasses. *How to begin?* "I know this is an odd question, Mom, but... was I adopted?"

Seeing her mother's shocked expression, she said, "I know I asked you repeatedly when I was young. Then it was because I don't resemble you or anyone else in the family. But something new has come up. Vic got me this Ancestry membership and DNA kit for Christmas." She explained it had revealed a Mediterranean heritage, with no trace of Swedish or Scottish lineage.

"It's wrong. That's all there is to it," Lilly said.

"A woman insists we're related. She's Greek."

"We're not Greek."

"No, Mother, but she and her family members live in West Virginia. That's where I was born, in some little coal town. It makes me wonder."

Lilly gave the long, drawn-out sigh of the forbearing.

"Eagle Energy took over a smaller company that operated over a dozen mines near Beckley. They moved us there from Chicago. Dreadful place, you may remember."

"I was three when we came to Pittsburgh. I remember nothing before that."

'The transition didn't go well," Lilly continued. "There was considerable tension between Eagle and the union. They brought your dad in to smooth things over. To build goodwill, he provided Thanksgiving dinner to every mining family that worked for them; it required us to attend three meals in three small towns, starting at ten in the morning."

Letting her reading glasses dangle on their cord, she rubbed her cheeks as though trying to force out the memory. "I was eight months pregnant at the time, but, dutiful wife that I am, I went along. We began in a high school gymnasium in a little town whose name I can't recall. Everything went well, despite considerable grumbling, but when your dad rose to welcome everyone, the miners began banging their utensils on the table. He shouted over them, 'Happy Thanksgiving, everyone,' and sat down. That shut them up."

Sarah leaned forward, resting her chin on her fists. She didn't recall having heard this story before. Lilly had hated her four years in Beckley and most likely had never wished to revisit them.

"Our second dinner was scheduled for one o'clock in a church hall. On our way, I went into labor and never made it. Your father continued the trip without me. You were born in a small clinic in Fessenden. When they brought you to me, I glanced at your wisps of strawberry blond hair and fell in love with you."

"I'd forgotten I was a blond baby," Sarah said.

"You've seen the pictures. You had a full head of hair by the time you were eight months, but it soon faded. By the time you were three, your head had turned this lovely brown color with auburn highlights, just as it is today."

Lilly smiled and took her hand. "You are mine, and I am yours. So you tell this woman, nicely, of course, that she's mistaken. And you," she said, her smile turning to a frown, "are twenty-eight—too old for such silly speculation."

As soon as she'd put Kellan down for his nap and cleaned the kitchen, Sarah opened her computer at the dining room table. She signed in to Ancestry and brought up Eleanor Frangos's message from the day before. She read it over twice, sat prayerfully before the screen while she considered what to say, and poured herself a cup of espresso to buy time.

"Dear Ms. Frangos," she wrote:

I have discussed your questions with my mother. She assures me we have no Greek ancestors. My father is a third-generation Swede. I have visited his family on Öland and Kalmar and even learned a bit of the language. My mother's family comes from Northern Ireland, but they have lived here for many generations. She is sure you and I are not related.

Ancestry seems to have mixed my DNA test with one of your relatives. I advise you to check with them.

While I respect your wish to reconstruct your family tree, I am not in a position to help you. I am extremely busy as a wife, mother, and host of "Sourdough Sal," my bread-baking channel on YouTube. I ask you, therefore, not to contact me again.

Once again, good luck with the search for your roots.

Sarah read what she had written, assuring herself that she had struck the proper balance between diplomacy and firmness. She considered eliminating the reference to her baking channel, but the marketer within her could not resist the chance to create another viewer.

Why am I wasting time on this woman? Wouldn't it be better just to leave her in suspense? She looked at the stack of fan letters she'd picked up from the post office this morning. She had not read comments on YouTube, answered emails, or checked orders on their website in two days.

No, she had to put a stop to these interruptions. She clicked the Send button, unaware she had made a strategic error.

With fewer than twenty hours left before she was to tape the next episode, Sarah had a problem—two, in fact. She had not yet perfected this recipe and had too little sourdough starter to do much testing. It took six ounces to make a single loaf of white bread. Multiply it by four—two for the dough demonstration and two for the beginning and finished loaves—and she needed twenty-four, plus at least three more to replenish the starter. She had only fifteen ounces and had to draw on this amount to test the recipe. Her fingers played a mock piano before her eyes as she thought. *I can use white flour and water as a stand-in for starter during the mixing scene; if Cheryl doesn't take a close-up, no one will be the wiser.*

But the recipe she was about to make must not fail. *How did I get so far behind?* As she assembled ingredients, the home phone rang. She was tempted not to answer it, but prospective clients sometimes reached Victor this way.

"Is this Sarah Mathews?" The woman's voice was unfamiliar, and the way she pronounced her name—*say-ra*—had an Appalachian spring to it.

"It is," she said.

Her caller paused so long Sarah thought she had disconnected. "This is Eleanor Frangos."

Sarah gasped as though a burglar had jumped out of the
shadows. "Ms. Frangos...,"

"It's *Mrs.* Frangos," she said in a tone that proclaimed the
last thing she wanted to be mistaken for was a feminist. "I'm
married."

"Mrs. Frangos, I don't know how you got my number,
but—"

"You wrote me about your bread thing on YouTube. I
looked you up. Your website mentions your husband is an
architect, and a friend at the library helped me find your
phone number." As she listened to the words, "a *fray-end at
the law-berry*," Sarah knew she'd done this to herself.

"This is an inconvenient time, and—"

"It'll only take a minute."

"It's totally inappropriate. I asked you not to contact me."

"Don't you want to hear about your family?"

Sarah took a deep breath while composing her response.
"I've told you; this is not my family. We are not connected."

She responded with a snort. "DNA don't lie." It was
almost a sing-song retort, as though they were two children
arguing on a playground.

"Perhaps not, but as I've explained, my results got mixed
up with someone else's."

"No one else in my family has taken the test. They will
now. I've arranged for my mother, her sister, and her daughter
to get tested."

"You're free to do that."

"Because if you're not theirs, that means you're the
daughter of my late brother."

"Mrs. Frangos, listen carefully. I am not a member of your
family. I have told you that at least three times now, yet you
persist in contacting me. This is harassment. If I hear from you

again—in writing, by phone, or in person—I will ask our family attorney to issue a restraining order. If you violate that, you will go to jail. Is that clear?"

"You can threaten me all you want, but if I get proof, you'll eat your words faster than a slice of your fancy bread."

With that, she hung up. Sarah leaned on the kitchen counter, resting her forehead on her tented fingers, her thumbs massaging her temples. Were someone to take her blood pressure at that moment, she was sure she'd be whisked to the emergency room at St. Clair Hospital.

Cheryl adjusted the soft light and ran the camera cables into her portable switcher. The overhead camera was permanently mounted, but they stored anything Kellan could reach in a locked cabinet. Still, studio set-up was easy; the equipment was lightweight, and Cheryl had marked tripod positions on the tile floor.

"Ready when you are," she said.

Sarah did not acknowledge her. She'd said little since Cheryl arrived and now stood with her hands on her hips, peering into the live stove just out of camera range. "What's wrong?" Cheryl said.

Sarah covered her mouth with her left hand. "It's not rising as it should. The whole wheat flour nearly burned up the machine, so I replaced about a quarter of it with bread flour, added some vital gluten, and increased the percentage of water. This made it too wet, almost like a whole wheat *ciabatta*, if there were such a thing."

"Didn't you test it?"

Sarah scowled at her. "There wasn't time. I'm contending with a lot of family stuff this week."

She pulled the loaf from the oven. It had collapsed in the

middle. She examined the unfinished loaf she'd pulled from the refrigerator two hours before. It, too, had deflated. "I thought if I transferred it carefully to the Dutch oven, the heat would make it rise, but you see what's happened."

One of the two bread machines stood before her on the counter's edge, along with the ingredients intended for the first scene. Off-set, a second machine was finishing its last rise. All was in readiness—all except the recipe. "I don't know what to tell you," Sarah said.

Cheryl shrugged. "It's no big deal. We're not under any deadline here. Take a few days, perfect the recipe, and we'll try again."

"I wonder if this is even possible. Whole wheat dough is too heavy for the bread machine. That's why I never use these things."

"Why not use a more powerful unit? This thing is so small."

"I've endorsed this brand. They're paying us for the exposure."

Cheryl knew little about baking, so she could suggest nothing more. What she did know was that this sloppiness was unlike her friend, who was usually so exacting in her preparations. "Why don't I remove the teaser from the last episode? We'll just pretend you never mentioned it."

"It's too late," Sarah said. "We've had over a thousand views; fans have posted messages saying how much they're looking forward to it."

"Why not record a different recipe and explain the whole wheat experiment didn't work?"

Sarah glowered at her. *Admit a mistake?* Cheryl thought. *Who do you think you're talking to?*

Sarah heaved a sigh. "I have to take some time off to deal with this family issue. Then I'll come back to this."

"Do you want to talk about it?"

The two women pulled stools up to either side of the counter as Sarah told her about the DNA test and the persistent woman who had tracked her down. "When she first contacted me, she seemed rational. The second time, she was insistent, a bit of an edge to her. Now she's become belligerent, and I don't know why."

Cheryl reached out for her friend's shaking hands, covering them with her own. "Why not take a new test and get your mother to take one, too?"

"I'll never convince her to do that."

"Sure you will. Look at me, working my ass off to make this gig a success instead of out looking for a new job. You can get anyone to do anything."

To her surprise, Lilly agreed to take the test. "Anything to put this behind us. I might discover I'm a descendant of the first Queen Elizabeth." She gave the matter a few seconds' thought. "Not her, I guess, but someone."

As Victor had suggested, Sarah deleted the first DNA test, paid for a second, and waited.

During the intervening two weeks, she adjusted the recipe by raising the percentage of white bread flour. Cheryl recorded the episode, and Sarah was careful not to tease anything specific at the end. Orders rolled in for the bread machine, rising baskets, aprons, sourdough starter, and all the other paraphernalia Sarah had dreamed up. Their YouTube subscribers had increased by fifty percent. Cheryl had posted short videos describing each step of their processes on their own website, sourdoughsal.com. Sarah could now capture her most devoted followers' names and email addresses for cross-marketing. She hadn't spent six years working for the region's leading marketing firm for nothing. She heard no more from

Eleanor Frangos and assumed her threat of legal action, which had been no bluff, had done its job.

On the last day of March, she received an email from Ancestry informing her that the new results were online. Giving a silent prayer, she signed in and clicked on the DNA link at the top left of the page. From the drop-down menu, she selected "Your DNA Results Summary."

A box appeared headed "Ethnicity estimate." She read the first line and felt her heart race. 62% Greek and Turkish, 21% Spanish and Portuguese, and 17% other regions. She clicked to expand this last group and saw a smattering of Italian, Macedonian, even Albanian.

What the hell? Despite the cold air seeping through the dining-room window, her skin flushed, and she began sweating.

If am not who I think I am, who in God's name am I?

Her email sounded an alert: "You have a new DNA match to explore." Before she could do so, a similar message appeared. She sat riveted before the keyboard, her hands knitted, wondering what to do.

Lilly. She had to alert Lilly. She reached for her cellphone but stopped, not knowing what to say.

"I'm so excited," Lilly said. "This is an adventure."

"I want you to be prepared for what you may find." Sarah had rushed to her mother's house as soon as she called but, preoccupied with what she'd uncovered, had no memory of driving there.

"What's wrong, dear? Your hands are shaking."

"Is Dad here?"

"No, he's at the office. That man never slows down. He has so much nervous energy."

Sarah longed for Steven's calm, reassuring support. She would have waited for his return had Lilly not insisted on seeing her results immediately.

"Show me how to get into this."

Sarah hesitated, trying to make this a slow reveal. She helped Lilly log in, showed her where the DNA menu was, and helped her navigate to her ethnicity estimate. With Sarah peering over her shoulder, they read the results: 52% Scotland, 32% England and Northwestern Europe. She opened the box with 15% other and found Germany, Spain, and Norway listed. "I wonder where the Spanish got in," Lilly said.

"England defeated the Armada," Sarah said. "Maybe a sailor washed ashore."

Lilly ignored the suggestion that there was anything untoward in her background. "And your results must look a bit like this."

Sarah leaned away from the screen and studied her mother, the straight, champagne color hair which showed hints of gray, straight features, and a large nose so unlike her own appearance. "No," she said.

"No?"

"Let me show you." Sarah opened a separate window and logged on to her account, showing Lilly her own estimate. "It's unchanged. I have no English blood, nor am I Scandinavian."

Lilly frowned. Her mouth dropped open. "That's impossible. There must be a mistake."

"It gets worse, Mom." Pulling down the DNA menu on Lilly's page, she selected DNA matches. "Here are all these people to whom you're related."

"There's my brother, Warren," Lilly said, "and his son and daughter. This is amazing."

When is she going to get it? "Who is missing, Mother?"

Lilly turned to her in confusion.

"Look at my DNA matches," Sarah said, returning to her results. "Who's missing from this picture?"

Her mother stared at the screen as the implications swept over her. She swiveled to face her daughter, an incredulous expression plastered on her face. Tears welled in her eyes. "But that's just wrong."

"It appears to be true."

"If you're not my daughter, who is?"

She returned to Lilly's screen. "It's this woman, Nora Bouras." And returning to her results, she said, "And the DNA says my birth mother is this woman, Virginia Bouras."

Lilly shook her head, denying what was displayed before her. "How could this have happened?"

"The Bourases live in Fessenden. Nora and I were born on the same day, and the town had only one small clinic back then."

Lilly's eyes switched from one half of the screen to the other. Sarah listened as she drew her breath in and out like an accordion.

"They switched us at birth, Mother."

Three

"HOW COULD THEY HAVE DONE THAT?" Lilly demanded in a strident tone. "It's not as though this piddly little clinic was awash in infants."

"It was a holiday," Sarah replied. "They may have been short-staffed. I doubt they were accustomed to having two babies born at the same time."

"You always look for the best in others," she said, cradling her coffee cup. "I hold people responsible for their actions."

One more way in which we differ, Sarah thought.

Lilly sat erect as she reached a decision. "I don't care. After all these years, it doesn't matter. I am your mother. No dots on a chart can change that."

Sarah reached over and hugged her. "And I am your daughter. Always have been, and always will be."

Lilly reached out and patted her on the head, taking advantage of the three-inch difference in their height. "My little girl," she said. "I waited so long for you. We had about given up hope."

"I know, Mom." She had heard her mother say this many

times. Disengaging from her mother's grasp, she said, "What will you do now?"

"What do you mean?"

Sarah stared at her, reluctant to speak. Did Lilly not grasp what she was asking?

"I'm going to go about my business as I always have. We're family. All this," Lilly said, waving her hand at the computer, "doesn't change a thing."

"Okay, Mom. That's good." Sarah logged off the Ancestry site and put the computer to sleep. *Is she in denial? Shock? Doesn't she realize this is about more than just the two of us?*

Her mother caressed the silver cross hanging from her necklace, a sure sign of distress. *She knows but doesn't want to deal with it. Soon, she'll have little choice. But, no matter what happens, I'll support her. Lilly is my mother.*

As she did at the end of each day, Lilly worked on her journal in the late afternoon, entering everything she could remember from the day. As she heard the garage door open, she stopped mid-sentence and set aside her work. Steven Lindstrom took the stairs two at a time, whistling a jazz tune as he always did. He doffed his suede jacket and hung it in the hall closet, then loped into the dining room and bent over his wife, planting a kiss on her forehead.

She grabbed his hand and held onto it. He pivoted around the table and fixed his gaze on her. "What's wrong?"

Lilly met his eyes, her brows knitted in concern. "You'd better sit down for this."

He lowered his six-foot three-inch frame into a chair across from her, resting his folded hands on the polished table. "Tell me."

All afternoon she had rehearsed how she would to break

this news to him. She had rejected the idea of calling him at his office, promising herself there would be no histrionics, just a flat recitation of the facts. But now, the words she had not wanted to say rushed out. "Sarah is not our daughter."

"What?"

"That is... She is our child, will always be, but she is not the baby I gave birth to."

He reached for her hand. "Lilly, what in God's name are you talking about?"

"Remember that Vic bought her a membership in that family tracking thing—"

"Ancestry."

"And a DNA test. When the results weren't what she expected, she retook the test and had me do the same. The results came back today. We're not related, Steven. She's someone else's child."

He spluttered a response. "Are you sure? These tests aren't one-hundred percent accurate. How do they know?"

She took him through Sarah's discovery and what they'd determined when comparing their results hours before. He listened, asking no questions. "I haven't thought about this in years, but I recall there was another woman in labor on that Thanksgiving Day," she said. "We suspect the nurses switched babies, bringing her daughter to me, and mine to her."

He ran both hands through his fading blond hair, his blue eyes wandering around the room. "We need to be certain before we draw any conclusions. Let me find a lab that specializes in genetic testing to confirm all this."

Lilly nodded her head, though in her heart, she knew what the results would be. Despite over two decades of assurances to her daughter, she had always known something wasn't quite right. Sarah was shorter than either of them, and her fingers were unlike her own long, graceful digits. Her meticulous nature was foreign to her and beyond Steven at his most persistent.

"I detest incompetence," Steven said. "The nurses at that little clinic should have been more careful, more thoughtful."

"Sarah suspects they were just short-staffed on the holiday."

"That's Sarah for you," he said, "ready to forgive anyone else's shortcomings."

"And she's still our little girl."

He nodded in agreement. "That she is, and that she always will be."

Two miles away, Victor struggled to make conversation with his wife, who sat in sullen silence, toying with her dinner. "I wish you'd never gotten me involved in that Ancestry nonsense," she said.

"I'm sorry. I thought it would be good for Kellan to know where he comes from."

"He's too young to know the difference. And when he's old enough, all I'll be able to serve him is a plate full of broken eggs."

"He'll have us," Victor said, unwilling to concede the point.

She plunged a knife into her plate of spaghetti, all she'd been able to come up with in the anger and confusion that had convulsed her afternoon.

"Besides, it was bound to come out." As she glowered at him, he forged on, knowing this was dangerous territory. "Genetic testing will soon be routine. Physicians are already using it to—"

"I don't give a damn how doctors use it. I'm talking about invading people's privacy."

"They're not doing that, honey."

"They certainly are."

Back and forth they went, their son sitting between them, turning his head from one to the other as though he were at a tennis match.

"I wish I'd never taken that test. It's changed everything I know about myself. It's—." She stopped mid-sentence, shaking her head.

He covered her hands with his. "You are still you. That's all that matters. You are Sarah Lindstrom Mathews, wife, mother, and entrepreneur. Nothing can change that."

She snorted and threw her napkin into her marinara sauce. "You really don't get it, do you?"

With that, Kellan burst into tears, ending the conversation.

Cheryl was about to leave her Brookline duplex when her cellphone chimed. Placing her travel mug on the entry table and laying her keys alongside it, she swiped her finger across the surface to answer it. "Yeah, I'm running late," she said without a greeting. "I'm leaving now."

"You can slow down," Sarah said. "I need to postpone."

"Okay," Cheryl said in a drawn-out voice, "but why?"

"It's a rye recipe, and I haven't prepared a starter. It'll take me a day or two to build it up. You okay for Monday or Tuesday?"

"I guess. I thought you were starting two days ago."

"Something got in the way. Sorry."

"Which day are you aiming for?" Cheryl asked.

She stood in the entry, staring at the pile of dirty, melting snow along the curb while she waited for an answer. The temperature was supposed to climb into the sixties by Sunday and into the mid-seventies during the coming week. Perhaps she could spend the free day getting her and Penny's bicycles out of storage and pumping up the tires.

"I guess Tuesday's okay," Sarah said.

Did she detect a lackadaisical tone in her friend's voice as she agreed to the revised date? "By the way, you were supposed to get me draft copy for the book last week. I have the editor on standby."

A long sigh. "I'm behind on that, too. Can she wait another week?"

Cheryl picked up her coffee mug and carried it back to the kitchen, draping her puffer jacket over the counter. "She's cleared this time for us. She has a pipeline, like any freelancer. If you're not ready, I'm sure she has another project in the wings, but we'll lose our place in line."

"I can't help it. I'm not ready."

"No need to yell at me. I'm just the messenger." Listening to the silence, she said, "Sarah, what's going on?"

"This DNA thing—it's gotten more complicated. I can't talk about it right now."

Hearing the anguish in her voice, Cheryl said, "Take your time. Get it straightened out. I'll take care of the editor. You take care of yourself. And if you need someone to talk to, I'm here."

"Thanks," Sarah said. "I may take you up on that."

White folks' problem, she thought as she disconnected, then caught herself. This was so unlike Sarah. Something must really be troubling her.

Meanwhile, she had to pay rent and put food on the table. For the first time, Cheryl questioned whether she'd made the right decision.

～

Sarah and Lilly spent two afternoons together over the week, and both families gathered for the traditional Sunday dinner, neither of them mentioning the DNA results. For the first few days, Sarah flinched whenever her home phone rang, expecting to hear Eleanor Frangos chortling about how she had been right all along. But she did not, and the email messages from Ancestry announcing "a new DNA match to explore" declined after the initial flurry. It was as though the question of Sarah's parentage had resolved itself; she and Lilly and Steven might not be related by blood, but they were still her parents. When they gathered for dinner after church on Sunday, Steven gave her a tight hug and held on to her for what seemed like a minute.

Sarah recorded the next episode but got lost in her narration as she lifted the risen dough from the proofing basket and placed it on a tile in the oven. This presented a problem, since she couldn't replace the dough without deflating it and marring the spiral pattern atop the loaf. Cheryl halted production while they discussed what to do. After reviewing the video to that point, she told Sarah to resume the narration while she aimed the camera at a side view of her face and promised to "fix it in post."

Sarah even made progress with the written introduction to the recipes they had selected for the book. As Cheryl had warned, however, the editor had moved on. Because they were self-publishing, this presented no other problem, save for delaying the launch of the long-promised print companion to the series.

While an air of normalcy pervaded her life, Sarah harbored no illusions. Having paid to test her aunt and three cousins, Eleanor Frangos was unlikely to let the matter rest. So she was not surprised when Lilly called the following Monday to ask for her help, telling her in a trembling voice that Ancestry had alerted her to a message.

Sarah was tempted to lead her through the few simple steps allowing her to access the message board on her own. Lilly might need her support, however. She dropped everything, scooped up Kellan and his battery of supplies, and arrived at her parents' home ten minutes later. "I want you to do this yourself," she said. "I'll guide you through it."

"All right." Lilly's voice conveyed her anxiety. She regarded the computer as a mystical presence, something that might envelop her if she touched the wrong key. The many lessons she'd taken at the senior center had done little to curtail her trepidation. It wasn't her age. Women a decade older were adept at spreadsheets and toured the internet as though it were a cruise ship. She just hated gadgets.

"Your username is your email address," Sarah said. "No, use an at sign, not a period here. Remember your password? Your password manager is that little box near the bottom of the screen. Just click there. It won't bite you, Mom. Now take the cursor over to the right-hand side of the screen...."

"Oh!" Lilly, who'd been hunched over the screen, recoiled. "It's from the girl, Nora."

"Are you going to open it?"

"Should I?"

Sarah turned to face her. "It's up to you, Mom. You can read it, ignore it, or set it aside while you think about it."

"It seems rude to ignore her, and I'm curious what she has to say." She looked at Sarah as though seeking permission.

"Your choice, Mom." *Once you do so, there's no turning back. But it's already too late. Victor cracked the door when he bought me the membership. I swung it wide when I asked you to take the test. Didn't it really start on Thanksgiving Day, 1994, when a nurse put the wrong baby into your arms?*

Both women held their breath as Lilly clicked on the link.

Dear Mrs. Lindstrom,

I hope I am not disturbing you. If so, please accept my apology. My Aunt Ellie insisted I take a DNA test a few weeks ago. It was her idea, not mine. As I'm sure you now know, it showed that you are my mother.

Needless to say, I was shocked to learn this. Virginia Bouras raised me and is as good a mother as any girl could ask. I love her very much and have never questioned my background.

I hope you'll understand, though, that I am curious about my biological heritage. Aunt Ellie says I need to learn as much of my family's medical history as possible for my own well-being. I am also eager to learn about you. Do I resemble you, sound like you, and think like you? All these things are exciting to learn, yet troubling, if you understand.

Would it be possible to talk by phone sometime? I don't want to upset you, but I would like to get in touch to learn whatever you're willing to tell me. If it's not too much trouble, please call me sometime. I would be most grateful and promise not to burden you.

She closed with a telephone number and a list of times she was available, which suggested to Sarah that she worked a night shift somewhere.

"She seems like a nice young woman," Lilly said, again looking at Sarah for approval.

"Yes, she does," she replied, although, to her, the woman had been obsequious. *Just tell her what you want and get it over with.*

"What should I do?"

"Mother, I can't advise you. You should write her back, but what you do next is your choice. You can call her and answer her questions, but you can also say you need time to process this or beg off, saying the situation is just too painful for you to deal with."

"It's not painful, though. It's upsetting for you, me, her, and, I'm sure, for her mother. But I'm not afraid of it. I think the right word is intrigued. Do you understand?"

"I do," Sarah said, although she could not bring herself to describe it in the same terms. Not yet, at least. "Whatever you do, Mother, I'll support you. But you have to decide."

"I'm going to call her," she said, nodding her head in vigorous agreement with her decision. "I owe her that much, at least."

Why do I feel like I've just been punched in the gut? "Right now?"

"Yes. Would you stay with me and listen?"

"No," she said, reaching for Kellan with one arm and his overstuffed diaper bag with the other. "You two need the chance to get to know each other. I'd feel like an intruder."

"That's not how I see it."

"I think it's best," she said. She drove two blocks, pulled to the side of the road, and waited until she'd dammed the tears welling in her eyes.

Four

SOUTH OF GASSAWAY, West Virginia, Interstate 79 veers west toward Charleston. To continue on to Beckley, Sarah exited to Highway 19, a divided highway interrupted at irregular intervals by traffic lights. "This is beautiful country," she said.

Sitting in the passenger's seat, Lilly sniffed. "I hate it. That's not a thing I often say, but this place holds no happy memories for me." Sarah kept her eyes on the road, knowing the rest of the story would emerge.

The pair were headed to the center of the state's mining industry to have lunch with Nora and Ginny Bouras, a meeting Nora had requested during two weeks of telephone conversations with Lilly.

Her mother had first welcomed the idea, but as the date approached, she became reluctant. "It's not the girl," she said. "I just don't want to go back there."

"It's difficult for Nora to visit us," Sarah had reminded her. "She works nights and is a single parent. If you want to meet her, this is the simplest way. And I'll drive."

Sarah had not spoken to Ginny, a stranger who just happened to be her birth mother, and was less invested in this meeting, but she would put no impediments in Lilly's way if meeting Nora was what she wanted.

"I had no friends here," Lilly said as a light rain began falling, "not one. These mining communities are tightly knit, and your father—Steven," she said, fumbling over how to describe their relationships as they both had for days now, "was management. I was incredibly lonely."

I'm sure you didn't make it easy on yourself, Sarah thought as the rain began pelting the windshield of her sporty BMW. While Lilly would bend over to help anyone, she did so from a sense of noblesse oblige, distinguishing between "we" and "they." She was a snob, to put it plainly, but seemed unaware of it.

"It will be over soon," Sarah said with an assurance she did not feel. She hunched over the steering wheel as the wiper blades churned ineffectually. "Shit!" she called, as a stopped tractor-trailer loomed ahead.

"You'd better slow down. They have traffic lights every mile or so along this stretch. Why they didn't put the Interstate through...."

Sarah said nothing as traffic crept forward. They cleared the squall as they approached the long bridge over the New River. A rainbow arched overhead, burying itself in the gorge below. Sarah took it as an omen, but Lilly took no notice. Overdressed in a knee-length, dark-blue dress with bright orchids, she bit her lip as they drove the last few miles, consumed by her private thoughts. As a mall approached, she directed Sarah past the ramp that would have taken them to Interstate 64 and onto the highway leading them into town. "Just a few blocks more," she said.

Minutes before noon, they pulled into the parking lot of a

chain steakhouse across the road from Walmart. A forest of Ford F-150s, Ram trucks, several SUVs, and a smattering of older cars of various makes filled the lot. Sarah parked between a curb and a handicapped spot, hoping to minimize the likelihood of a truck door slamming into the side of her BMW though not, she knew, of being keyed.

They entered the open lobby and found three women sitting on a bench facing the cash register. Two appeared to be in their late forties or early fifties, dark-haired, tired-eyed, and overweight, but the younger woman between them arrested Sarah's attention. While nearly three decades separated them, her resemblance to Lilly was chilling—the same straight blond hair, deep blue eyes, a slightly prominent nose, and a long, swanlike neck. Everything she was not. Any remaining doubts about the accuracy of Ancestry's DNA results fled.

Smiling, Lilly extended her hand to the young woman. "You must be Nora."

She returned the smile and, in a soft voice, introduced the older women, "Virginia, my mother, and Cousin Ellie."

"Call me Ginny," the younger of the pair said. Sarah introduced herself, clasping Ginny's hands in hers but only nodding to Eleanor Frangos, whose presence was an unwelcome surprise.

"Let's get seated," Eleanor said. "This place gets busy at lunchtime, and they won't hold our booth forever. Barb," she called to the cashier, "these folks have come all the way from Pittsburgh to see us."

The woman led them to a curved booth near the salad bar flanking the back wall. Eleanor slid into the middle of the booth and motioned Lilly to follow her. "Nora, you sit next to her. Ginny, slip in on my other side, and you," she said to Sarah, "sit on the outside, next to her."

The four did as they were told. Nora asked how their trip

had gone, but Eleanor overrode her. "The steaks here are excellent, particularly the ribeye. But if you don't eat meat, their fried chicken is good, too."

Sarah and Lillian studied the menu, but the other three closed theirs. They were well acquainted with the restaurant or had read the menus while waiting in the lobby. The server set glasses of ice water before them and asked if they wanted to order beverages. "Bourbon and branch," Eleanor said, without waiting for the others. "Go easy on the ice."

Nora and Ginny ordered Bud Lights. Lilly asked what wines were available. "They're on the back," the server said. Sarah flipped over the menu and saw they served two reds and three whites, all by a label for whom the term *vin ordinaire* was a stretch. They settled for the Sauvignon Blanc, which Sarah figured was safest.

Eleanor ordered her steak, her relatives chose meatloaf, and Lilly and Sarah settled on shrimp salads. That done, Sarah studied Nora as she chatted with Lilly, speaking in such a low, lilting tone that Sarah couldn't hear a word. Even Lilly leaned closer to listen to her. As she spoke, her hands danced in the air, long, graceful fingers describing whatever she was saying.

Trying to bridge the length of the semi-circular table, Sarah said, "Nora, I hear you also have a son. How old is he?"

Without turning, Eleanor, who sat with her back to Sarah, reached out her arm to silence her with an imperious wave. The rude gesture so stunned her that Sarah said nothing. She sat at the end of the table as a banal conversation wore on, Eleanor prodding it with suggestions like, "Tell her about how you won the all-state basketball tournament."

Their meals arrived. The three women dived in, Eleanor sawing at her steak with so much effort it confirmed to Sarah why the other two had settled on meatloaf. Their plates were brimming with food—meat, mashed potatoes, and a "vegetable medley," as the menu would have it, that appeared to have been poured from a can. Lilly picked at her salad while Sarah took a few bites and laid down her knife and fork. The room had filled up, and the noise level was so loud Sarah could hear none of the conversation at the opposite end, except for Eleanor's loud effort to direct the conversation.

Sarah tried to banter with Ginny, but the woman answered in monosyllables. Finally, she said, "This must be quite a shock for you."

Ginny nodded, then said, "But something didn't seem right from the moment she was born. Paulie—that was my husband—he took one look at her and said, 'You sure that's our baby?'"

"Did you have doubts yourself?"

"Not really. I had two other kids after her—one year apart. I didn't have time to think about it." She returned to her food as though the conversation was closed.

"Paulie is my father?"

Her nod was less vigorous this time. "Was. He died while Nora was in high school."

"I'm sorry to hear that." She waited for Ginny to provide details, and when she didn't, asked, "What sort of man was he?"

The woman studied her for a moment, then turned back to her food. "He was a good man, hard-working, a devout Christian." She paused for a beat. "Are you saved?"

Am I saved? "I attend the Presbyterian Church in Upper St Clair. Mom—Lilly is a deacon. She used to chair the board."

"Oh," Ginny said, as though the answer was insufficient.

"How did Paulie die?"

Again, Ginny peered at her, a searching look that made her think she'd asked something inappropriate. "They said it was an accident," she said. Another subject seemed closed.

Ginny asked no questions of Sarah, displaying no curiosity about her birth daughter's life. Nor did she attempt to keep the conversation going. It was almost as though she didn't want to be there. "Your cousin seems to be enjoying herself," Sarah said.

"She is. This was her thing, you know. Ellie got interested in all this roots business through Dr. Gates's program on public TV. Never misses it. She started looking into our family and—here we are."

"And you? Are you curious about it?"

Ginny tossed her napkin into the congealed gravy on the plate. "I'm sorry all this got started," she said in a low voice. "We had our family and knew who we were to each other. We were living our lives. And now this. Some things are better left alone, don't you think?"

Sarah nodded. "I agree."

"How about dessert?" Eleanor bellowed. "The chocolate cake here is delicious."

Sarah and Lilly demurred, but Eleanor was insistent. "Laura," she said to the server, "bring us a couple pieces of chocolate cake with vanilla ice cream on the side. And five spoons. And coffee. Does everyone want coffee?"

On that, they could agree. While they waited, Eleanor began holding forth about the town's history. "A Mr. Beckley named the town after himself, only there was no town back then. It was a big joke. And now, look at it. Before you leave, visit the coal mine exhibit. It's our big tourist attraction."

"Some other time, perhaps," Sarah said. "I have to get back to make my son's dinner."

The desserts arrived, and despite her good intentions, Sarah had a taste. Eleanor was right. It was delicious. Someone knew what they were doing. She considered asking for the recipe, but vetoed the idea.

"It is so great we can all get together as a family," Eleanor said as they stood in the lobby, gathering their jackets around them. "We'll have to do this again real soon."

Nora reached out to Lilly and hugged her, a gesture Lilly returned, murmuring something in the younger woman's ear. Sarah shook hands with the three women, not failing to notice the smug expression on Eleanor's face as she did so. Nor did it escape Sarah's attention that no one but Lilly had reached for the check.

~

"I wish I'd brought Kellan with me," Sarah said. "I would have had someone to talk to."

"That bad?" Victor said. They sat at their dining table, eating Chinese carry-out he had picked up after she declared she was too worn out to cook.

"Worse," she answered as she picked up a tablespoon of white rice in her hand, squeezed it into a ball, and put it on Kellan's tray. "Eleanor—Nora's cousin, the one who started all this—planted herself at the center of the booth, turned her back on me, and directed the conversation with Lilly and Nora. The one time I tried to engage with Nora, she shushed me."

Kellan stuffed the rice ball into his mouth and reached for another. "I couldn't get Ginny to open up," she said as she fashioned Kellan a second and a third. "She seemed embarrassed to be there, said things like this should be left alone, but that was all I got out of her. I felt like the proverbial fifth wheel."

"I'm sorry you had to go through this," he said, "but it's over and done with."

"Don't bet on it. As we were making our getaway, Eleanor announced she wants us to meet again. 'Real soon,' she said."

Victor gave a partial shrug. "Just because she asks for it doesn't mean you have to give it to her."

"She who must be obeyed," Sarah said, giving a derisive snort.

"And Lilly?" he said between mouthfuls of fish in leek sauce. "How did she take this?"

His wife laid down her chopsticks and looked off into the distance. "The way Eleanor set things up, I couldn't see her face, but she was listening to everything Nora said, nodding and encouraging her. On the drive home, she was quiet for the first ten minutes, like she was lost in thought. When I asked if she'd enjoyed herself, her face lit up. 'Oh, yes,' she said."

She repeated the phrase with a mournful quality. "'Oh, yes. She seems like such a nice young woman, but she's had a hard life.' Once Lilly opened up, there was no stopping her. They only spoke for an hour or so, but she chattered all the way to the Pennsylvania line—what Nora did in high school, how her father's death required her to go to work, shelving her plans to attend WVU."

"Was she upset over Eleanor's treatment of you?"

Sarah crossed her right arm under her breasts and massaged her forehead with her left hand. "She didn't even notice, Victor. I said something about Eleanor's pushiness, and she defended her. Said she was just being helpful. At that moment, I felt so—" and here she whispered the word *Goddamn* "—alone."

"I know how you must feel," he said.

"No," she said, "you don't."

"I only mean...."

"I know what you mean. You're trying to be helpful, and I appreciate it. But you cannot understand how I feel. No one can."

He was silent for a moment, not knowing how to respond to the outburst. "We had a good day," he said, changing the subject. "A new client asked me to inspect his property in Peters, across Chartiers Creek. I almost begged off, but I took Kellan with me. You should have seen him. The weather was glorious. He took off across that field like a pony, didn't you, Buddy?"

Kellan smiled and laughed. "Pony!" he shouted.

"Yeah, we'll get you on a pony one of these days. You with me?" he asked her.

Blinking, she turned to him as though awakened. "I hope you held on to him."

Victor didn't get what she meant at first, then realized she hadn't been paying attention. "Of course," he said. If she thought Kellan had taken his first pony ride, he wasn't about to argue the point. "And Steven? What does he think of all this?"

"He's in shock, like the rest of us, but you know how cautious he is. He didn't want us going today. 'Give it time,' he said. 'Don't rush into this.'"

"Good advice."

"Very," she said, rising from the table and carrying her half-eaten meal to the sink.

After scraping grains of rice off Kellan's tray, he followed her with his dish. "And you?" he said. "How will you handle this?"

She took the plate from him, rinsing it in the sink before placing it in the dishwasher. "I'm going to do what I've done for twenty-eight years, be a devoted daughter."

Having not heard from Sarah in days, Cheryl called on the first Monday in May with what she hoped was good news. "Our editor just wrapped up a novel she was working on and is ready for us. If we're ready for her," she added.

"When does she need it?" Sarah said.

"She's ready now. I'm sure I can buy a few days, but by Wednesday." Met with silence, she said, "Is that possible?"

"I need more time," came the response.

"How much?"

"I don't know," Sarah replied with evident impatience. "I'm working on it, along with a lot of other things."

"We agreed I would finish changes to our website while you worked on the copy."

"I'm sorry."

"Sarah, I have nothing else going for me right now. I've put all my chips on black."

"I know you have," Sarah responded in a sympathetic tone.

Cheryl waited. Her partner owed her something more than a mere acknowledgment.

"My mother—Lilly is spending hours talking with Nora. They phone each other. They FaceTime. They email back and forth. I have no idea what they're saying to each other, what they're planning."

This isn't my problem, and I'm not a psychologist, Cheryl thought. "Perhaps they're not planning anything," she said. *Then again, she's making this my problem, and I'd better play counselor.* "You need to let this thing play its course. You've said yourself they have nothing in common other than the blood relationship. She's a warehouse worker from a poor, rural community. Your mother is...?"

"An aristocrat," Sarah said. "At least, that's how she acts."

"Exactly. So listen, be supportive, but live your life. You can't change what's happened. It isn't your doing."

"I know," Sarah said, reverting to her refrain.

"And that means protecting the business. We're on a roll. We need to focus. Both of us."

Cheryl heard heavy breathing come through the phone, as

though Sarah was hyperventilating. "I'll go to work on it now," she said. "I'll have the copy to you by noon Wednesday."

She thanked her and hung up, wondering whether this pledge would be any more binding than the last.

~

Sarah was huddled over her computer when her cell phone rang. "Hi, Mom."

"Are you busy?" Lilly asked.

"I'm working on my cookbook. Cheryl needs copy in the morning, and I'm way behind. Viv has taken Kellan to the park so I can finish."

"This will just take a minute." It was typical of her mother to pose a question but ignore the answer. Having never worked for a living, she recognized neither timelines nor deadlines. "I just got off the phone with Nora. She's coming for a visit."

Sarah hit save and closed the display. "When is this?"

"Saturday. Eleanor is driving her up."

"Terrific," Sarah said, barely masking her sarcasm. "How long will she stay?"

"She didn't say. About a week, I think."

"You think?"

"What's wrong? You're eager to see her, aren't you?"

"I'm sorry, Mom. I'm preoccupied with this project." Sarah forced herself to brighten her tone. "It's great news. I'm excited for you."

"I'll need your help," Lilly said. "I want to show her the skyline from Grandview Overlook, let her ride the Mon Incline, and take her to the Andy Warhol Museum. I wonder if the symphony is playing on Sunday. Can you check? She needs to see everything."

"Maybe she'll want to go shopping while she's here," Sarah said.

"Of course. I should have thought of that. There are no decent stores in Beckley. You'll take her, won't you?"

"Sure, Mom. Whatever you want. I'm happy to help." Sarah enjoyed shopping, so this part of the visit would be a lark. And it would allow her to monitor whatever Lilly and Nora were discussing. *Not that I'm snooping*, she told herself.

"The two of you can get better acquainted. You said you didn't have time to talk much in Beckley. Maybe she can spend a day or two with you."

Even better. "That's fine. It will give Victor a chance to meet her, too."

"And Steven. This will be good for all of us."

"Is Dad excited about the visit?" Sarah said.

"He doesn't know yet. I wanted to tell you first. But you know him. He'll be fine with it."

"I'm sure. How long will her aunt stay?"

"She'll probably turn right around and drive back." Sarah doubted that. She hoped Eleanor didn't intend to hang around, eavesdropping and controlling the conversation. "Nora doesn't have a car, and the bus trip takes eight hours," Lilly added. "It goes by way of Columbus. Do you believe that?"

"I do," Sarah said. "Well, good news, Mom. I look forward to it. But right now, I have to get back to work."

"You work too hard, dear."

"I'm fine, Mom. I enjoy it, and it gives me a purpose."

"I'd think Victor and Kellan are purpose enough."

"Goodbye, Mom. I love you." She hung up before Lilly could take the conversation in a new direction.

She opened the computer again, but instead of resuming her work, she stared at the screen, resting her mouth and nose on knitted fists. Lilly wanted to get to know the woman to whom she had given birth. Sarah understood that. If the same thing had happened to her, she would want the same thing. *I'm the first person she called, and she's including me in every-thing. I must be there for her, but I'll be here to protect her if it becomes necessary. This will all work out.*

Five

AN EVENING BREEZE stirred the leaves of the Japanese maple as Lilly and Steven sat on their enclosed deck, enjoying their cocktails and the view of their spacious lawn which rolled down the hill toward the stream running behind their property. Steven had made her a cosmopolitan and a gin and tonic for himself. A family of cardinals clustered around the bird feeder, the younger ones having fledged three days before.

It was, she thought, a tranquil atmosphere in which to raise a sensitive subject. "We have a visitor coming."

"Oh?" he said. He sat on a lounge chair, his moccasins crossed over each other at the end of his long legs.

She waited for him to ask who, but when he didn't, she said, "Nora is coming up on Saturday to stay with us for a few days."

He frowned, scowling at her over his dark glasses. "Did you invite her?"

"No," she said. "No, she called this morning and said she'd like to come—"

"She invited herself, in other words."

"She was sweet about it, said she'd never been to Pittsburgh before and would like to spend a few days with us." He took a sip of his drink without replying. "You don't want her to come?"

"It's not that. I just think it's premature."

"In what way?" Unused to disagreements with her husband, Lilly tried to keep the tension out of her voice.

"We hardly know the woman. You were just down there, and suddenly she wants to come for…. How long is she staying?"

"Just a few days, I think."

If he noticed her uncertainty, he didn't say so. "It's rather sudden is all. You said her father is dead. What did he do?"

Steven peppered her with questions, the answers to which she didn't know. "We can ask her all that when she arrives," she said. "In the end, it doesn't make much difference, does it?"

"I suppose not. Do you want a refill?"

Lilly did not, but Steven rose to pour himself a second drink, something he rarely did before dinner. He was taking this badly, and she sensed it was her fault. When he returned a moment later, she said, "I should have asked you first. I'm sorry."

"Don't be. She put you in a spot. What were you supposed to say?"

"This will give you a chance to meet her. I'm sure you'll like her. She's a very pleasant young woman." When he didn't answer, she said, "I'm sure you're curious about her, aren't you? She is our flesh and blood. You'll see it the moment you set eyes on her."

"Just don't forget about Sarah. We mustn't make her feel left out."

"She doesn't. She's helping me plan the visit—what to see, where to eat."

"Good," Steven raised his glass in a toast to his daughter. "She's a trooper."

He reached out and patted her knee. "I'm a cautious person. You know that. And the biggest reason for my concern is Sarah's welfare. If she feels comfortable and it's what you want, I'm all for it."

Sarah pulled an all-nighter and got copy for the cookbook to Cheryl by early Wednesday morning. Vivian had classes at Pitt, so Sarah lurched through the morning, making breakfast for the three of them, then tending to Kellan. By early afternoon, she was so exhausted she took Kellan to bed with her for his afternoon nap, so she'd awaken when he did. He slept for an uncharacteristic two hours, and when she awoke, she found him curled up alongside her, rubbing her arm.

She turned in early that night, having lost a day of preparations for Nora's visit. Victor watched over their son for an hour so Sarah could get to Trader Joe's. She returned with three lamb racks, which she marinated in a mixture of chopped onions and garlic, lemon juice and honey, curry, cayenne, and mustard powder.

Over the next forty-eight hours, Sarah made reservations at the Carnegie Art and Warhol Museums and at Falling Water, the Frank Lloyd Wright House in Mill Run. She also reserved a table at Altius, a favorite restaurant overlooking the city near the Duquesne Incline. She planned luncheons and dinners and, in typical fashion, recorded excursions and meals in her daily planner, down to what groceries she would have to purchase, where, and when.

Lilly wouldn't have to lift a finger. Sarah had arranged everything, ensuring that she and Lilly could spend time with Nora unencumbered.

In this way, she put her fears of dispossession out of her mind and began anticipating Nora's arrival. "I always wanted a sister when I was growing up," she told Victor over dinner Friday evening. "All my friends came from these big families. They had someone looking after them and someone to look after. I just had myself. Perhaps I'm getting my wish."

Thus, when she arrived at Steven and Lilly's home on Saturday, she was in a buoyant mood. She took Kellan from his car seat, entering the kitchen via the side door into the garage as she always did. Her son rushed to hug both his grandparents. Lilly took him off to play while Steven helped Sarah bring in the lamb, black rice, fresh spring asparagus, and the 1886 Chocolate Cake from Austin's Driskill Hotel. "Have you heard from them?" she asked.

"No," Lilly said, "but relax. They said they'd be here around three, and it's just turned two-thirty." Sarah busied herself in the kitchen, chopping garlic and greens for the rice dish and trimming asparagus spears, which she covered in water in a sauté pan. She removed the lamb from the marinade and placed it in a large enameled baking dish. Steven brought up two bottles of pinot noir from the wine cellar.

All was in readiness except the guests. Three o'clock came and went, then four o'clock with no word. Lilly, who earlier had tried to calm Sarah, paced back and forth at the entrance, kneading her hands. "Do you think something's happened to them?"

"I'm sure they're just running late," Steven said.

"Maybe they got lost."

"If so, they'll call."

Sarah suppressed the temptation to point out it would have been common courtesy to do so anyway. She saw no point in adding to Lilly's anxiety. "They'll be here," she said.

As though on cue, a red Ford F-150 pulled into the circular driveway. Lilly and Sarah emerged to greet them, with

Steven trailing behind. As Nora emerged from the passenger side of the truck, Lilly exclaimed, "You're late. We've been worried."

"We got a late start," Eleanor said as she came around the truck bed.

Nora embraced Lilly, shook hands with Sarah, and gaped at the sprawling contemporary L-shaped house, with its three garages to the right, multi-tiered living area to the left, and large plate-glass windows dominating its stone exterior. "Wow!" she said.

Lilly introduced her to Steven, and she gave him a quick hug. "I don't know what to call you," she said in a voice so low Sarah could barely hear it.

"Steven will do. That's what Sarah calls me."

He introduced himself to Eleanor, who stood observing the scene with her hands on her hips. "You want to give us a hand with these suitcases?" she said.

He grasped the heavier of the two while Sarah grabbed the roll-aboard. Lilly led the two guests inside, while Sarah and Steven trailed behind them. As they entered the front door, Nora peered up at the glass chandelier suspended over the two-story foyer as it reflected the late afternoon sun. "This is mind-blowing," she said, her hands reaching out to encompass all she saw. "I've never seen a place this big."

"We bought it from a couple who'd only lived in it a year," Lilly said. "The husband died suddenly, and his widow was so eager to get rid of it, she made us a great deal."

"They don't need to know all this, dear," Steven said.

Sarah cringed. Why did Lilly feel the need to apologize? Steven had worked hard for what he had.

Hearing their voices, Kellan came running from the family room, where he'd been playing with a plastic fire truck Steven had bought him. "I'm Kellan," he told the two women. "This mommy."

Nora knelt to shake his hand. "I'm Nora," she told him.

Kellan parroted her. "Noah," he said, grinning.

"How old is he?" Nora asked, and when Sarah told her he was nearly two, she shook her head. "And speaking already?"

Lilly asked Sarah to show Nora to her room. As she led the woman up the stairs, the aunt followed. "Mom is putting you in my room," Sarah said. "I'm afraid it still looks like it did when I got married." Posters of Beyoncé, Lorde, and Taylor Swift adorned the pink walls. Bold stripes in pink and white ran across the ceiling. A light pink comforter covered the white four-poster bed, which was bracketed by matching end tables. A white bookcase held volumes from *Peter Pan* and *From the Mixed-Up Files of Mrs. Basil E. Frankweiler* to college textbooks.

"This is fine," Nora said. "Thanks."

"And where are you putting me?" Eleanor said.

"You're staying the night?"

"What do you think? It's too late to drive home."

"We have a guest room. Dad uses the fourth bedroom for a home office."

"'Dad?'" Eleanor said in an accusatory tone. "I thought you call him Steven."

"Most of the time, I do." Sarah offered no further explanation, refusing to rise to the challenge.

After showing Eleanor the room, she returned to the lower level and grabbed one of the two heavier suitcases. "I'll do that," a familiar voice behind her said. She turned to see her husband standing at the front door.

"Glad you're here," she whispered in Victor's ear.

"The same thing as in Beckley?" Victor said.

"Nora's pleasant enough. It's her little auntie who seems out for a fight."

"Nothing little about her," he whispered as he looked up the staircase at the figure hovering over them. "Hello, there.

I'm Victor, Sarah's husband. And Kellan is... gone." He finished his sentence with a chuckle.

He picked up the heavy suitcase and balanced it over his head as he climbed the stairs. Sarah followed, dragging the smaller one after her. Victor introduced himself to Nora, who favored him with a hug. "I've heard so much about you," she said in her lilting voice.

"Oh?"

"Eleanor found me through you," Sarah said.

"I'm glad she did," Victor said. "Welcome."

The three of them headed downstairs and found Steven, Lilly, and Eleanor on the deck, drinks in hand. Kellan sat on the tile flooring, dangling a plastic mouse above Clarence, the family cat, who appeared not to notice as he lazed in the afternoon sun.

Steven offered to mix more drinks. "I'll pass," Sarah said. "I need to prepare dinner." She retreated to the kitchen, grateful for the diversion. She sautéed the garlic and green onions and heated chicken stock, adding equal amounts of black and brown rice once it simmered. Then she turned on the oven and inserted a thermometer into the heaviest of the three lamb racks. While she waited for the rice to cook, she reached into the refrigerator and poured herself a glass of white Burgundy from the open bottle.

"How are you doing, Kitten?"

"I'm fine," she told Steven. "How's it going out there?"

"I rather like Nora, but her aunt is overbearing. She constantly interrupts, answering for her whenever we pose a question."

"Tell me about it." Steven raised his gin and tonic and clicked it against her wine glass. "She'll be gone tomorrow, and we can get to know Nora for ourselves."

"I hope you're right," he said. "If not, I'm moving in with

you two." He returned to the deck, carrying the open bottle with him.

With the rice almost done, she added the garlic and onions, stirred to combine them, and checked the lamb's temperature. She painted their surfaces with hoisin sauce, then topped a salad of spinach and hard-boiled eggs with toasted *pignoli* and goat cheese and poured lemon vinaigrette over it. She pulled the lamb from the oven to let it rest as she boiled the asparagus in a half cup of water, finishing them with two tablespoons of butter as it evaporated.

Victor split the lamb chops. "You've outdone yourself."

They carried the platter and bowls of food to the table. Steven, who was filling wine glasses, stopped mid-pour. "No," he told Eleanor. "That's Sarah's seat."

The woman paused, holding the place cards she had been switching in her hand. "I think Nora should sit here," she said.

"Dad, I don't mind."

"No," he said. "Sarah sits to the left of me, Lilly to my right. It's always been that way, and I'm not about to change it."

"O-o-okay," Eleanor said, as though she were giving in to a petulant child.

Five of them sat in embarrassed silence as Steven gave the blessing, welcoming Nora into their home and praying for Eleanor's safe return, an irony not lost on Sarah. If Steven knew he was being unreasonable, he gave no sign of it. *He's been out listening to her for the past half-hour,* she thought. *Perhaps he's had his fill of her, as have I.*

As the plate passed in front of Eleanor, she said, "What is this?"

"It's lamb," Lilly said. "Sarah makes it better than anyone, even better than high-end restaurants."

"I don't eat lamb," she said.

Hearing Steven's intake of breath, Sarah placed a

restraining hand on his arm. "I made a chicken lasagna last night. I can heat some for you."

"Fine," she said.

As she rose from the table, Steven couldn't restrain himself. "More of this delicious meat for the rest of us. Sarah's worked all week on this."

"Lamb, Daddy," Kellan hollered, putting an exclamation point on the exchange.

~

"That was some scene," Victor said as he took the short drive to their house.

"It was embarrassing."

"For whom, your dad or what's-her-name?"

"It's Eleanor, and I was embarrassed for Dad."

"Not me. I was proud of him. The man knows how to stand his ground."

She thought for a moment and chuckled. Soon, they both laughed, Kellan joining in from the back seat.

"Man, when he gets pissed...," Vincent said.

They pulled into their garage, and Vincent carried Kellan off to his bath while Sarah moved the plates and insulated bag into the kitchen.

"Nightcap?" he asked when he'd put the boy down for the night.

"No," she said. "Hell, yes. We've earned it."

He poured two small servings of ice wine. She lifted the sweet liquid to her nose, inhaled, then took a sip. "Glad that's over," she said. "Tomorrow, we're rid of her and can spend a week getting to know Nora."

"Hm."

"You like her, don't you? She's not like that aunt of hers."

"Not at all, but her oohing and ahhing got a bit old."

"But she said herself, she's never seen a home like this."

"I suppose so," he said. "She seemed envious."

"More, please." Sarah extended her glass. As Victor refilled it, she said, "Perhaps she is. But don't you think she has a right to be? If not for the carelessness of one nurse, all this would have been hers. And I would have grown up in a West Virginia coal town."

"And we," he said, "would never have met. Which makes me think that with Kellan asleep and the dishes done, we could get to know each other better."

"Down the hatch," she said, upending her glass and leaving it behind as she mounted the stairs.

Eleanor's game of musical chairs continued Sunday morning. Sarah arrived at the Lindstrom house with Kellan in hand, bringing a loaf of bread as she often did, ready to join Lilly and Steven for church. Victor had backed out, preferring to spend the sunny morning with three friends pursuing white balls across grass and through trees and bunkers. The four stood in the kitchen, joined by Nora, who wore a black dress with white polka dots. "You look nice," Sarah said.

"Thanks. I bought this special for the trip from a consignment store in Beckley."

Sarah winced at Nora reminding them she had grown up in straitened circumstances. "Where's Eleanor?" she said.

"She's not coming. She's decided to stay and rest up."

Steven pulled his chin in. "I'll do the same."

"But you never miss church." Lilly's voice was just short of a whine.

"I know, but today, I'm going to stick around and get some work done."

As he stood dressed in his blue serge wool suit with

matching vest, it was clear to Sarah this was a last-minute decision, and Nora sensed it, too. "Let me have a word with Aunt Eleanor," she said, mounting the stairs. "She ought to come with us."

"Make it snappy," Steven said, "or we'll be late."

Five minutes later, both women descended the staircase, Eleanor dressed in a black satin dress with puffy sleeves. She had pulled her dark hair to one side as though she'd run a brush and comb through it at the last minute. In her haste, she tripped on the last stair and would have sprawled on the terrazzo floor had Steven not caught her. She glared at him. "Are we ready?" she said.

"For some time," he replied, making a show of checking his watch.

The organist had already begun the prelude by the time Steven ushered them into the sanctuary. He stood to one side directing traffic—Eleanor first, then Nora, Lilly, Sarah, and Kellan—before taking his seat at the end of the pew.

Associate Pastor Dana Warren issued the welcome and made a few announcements, then led the congregation in the call to worship. The organist introduced the first hymn, "Praise Ye the Lord, the Almighty," playing a powerful variation on the last verse as the sopranos added a descant. Kellan fidgeted as Pastor Warren led the prayer of confession, followed by a moment of silence. When she closed it with a single "Amen," Nora and Eleanor echoed her words. Steven bent forward to peer down the row, but Sarah stopped him with gentle pressure on his left arm. As the congregation joined the choir in singing the Gloria Patri, Kellan squirmed out of Sarah's arms and began tugging at his grandfather's shoelaces while speaking to him in a loud voice. Scooping him up, Sarah headed for the cry room, following the rest of the service as best she could while Kellan wandered about, trying to awaken two infants sleeping in their carriers.

She rejoined the family as they left the church, bringing about the first awkward moment when Lilly struggled to introduce the two strangers to the senior pastor, Ray Hillebrand. "These are...," she began.

In the ensuing pause, Steven said, "Good friends from West Virginia, Nora Bouras and Eleanor Frangos."

The minister welcomed them and said he hoped to see them again. "Oh, you will," Eleanor replied.

Once in the car, no one spoke until Eleanor broke the silence. "What's for dinner?"

"You mean now?" Lilly said. "Sarah is making us a tuna salad."

"Salad Niçoise," Sarah corrected. "We get the best albacore from this little shop in Seaside, Oregon. I order it by the case."

Eleanor sniffed. "We usually have our big sit-down after church on Sunday. And I have to get on the road in a while."

"There's a nice little restaurant in Mount Lebanon," Sarah said.

Steven said nothing but drove past the side road that would have taken them to their neighborhood. He drove another mile and turned right onto Fort Couch Road, passing a shopping mall. Sarah tried to catch his eye in the rear-view mirror, but he gazed at the road ahead with grim determination, turning into the parking lot of an Eat' n Park, a local chain restaurant known more for its quantity than its quality.

"Good, solid food," he said, "to tide you over before you arrive home."

Eleanor had one more surprise awaiting her when the server approached the table to take their drink order and responded to her request by saying, "We don't serve alcohol."

~

After handing Kellan over to Vivian for the afternoon, Sarah picked up Nora and Lillian to visit the Andy Warhol Museum on the North Side. Both sat in the back seat, leaving her feeling like their chauffeur as she drove north on I-79 to its intersection with the Parkway West. As they emerged from the Fort Pitt Tunnel, Nora got her first glimpse of the Pittsburgh skyline. "My God," she said.

She proved to be less impressed by the museum, breezing past the solarized Marilyn Monroe images without comment and staring at the painting of a Campbell's Soup can. "What is that?" she said.

Sarah tried to explain the technique Warhol used. "But it's just a can of soup," Nora said, her mouselike voice taking on an edge. "What's the point?"

"No one had ever treated ordinary manufactured objects as art until Andy came along," Sarah explained. "A friend suggested he paint something ordinary, creating art from an everyday object. He loved Campbell's soup, so he chose the can as his subject, creating the Pop Art movement. He's buried a few miles from our house. People leave soup cans at his gravestone."

Nora shrugged. "It's just a can of soup."

They left the museum early. Sarah drove them home after a quick tour past Heinz Field and PNC Park, homes to the Steelers and Pirates. As the two women chatted in the back seat, Sarah tried to join in, but gave up because they had difficulty hearing her.

To her, the day had been a washout. She'd felt isolated during the drives to and from the museum, but tried not to show it. Scolding herself for being self-absorbed, she realized that if she felt ignored, Ginny Bouras must feel twice as bad. After giving Kellan his bath and tucking him into bed, she gave the woman a call.

After identifying herself, she told how they'd spent the past two days. "But I'm sure she's told you all this," Sarah said.

"No, I haven't talked to her. I know she's busy."

Sarah tried to describe the Warhol Museum, crediting Nora with more interest than she'd displayed. Ginny muttered "Uh-huh" a few times but expressed no more interested than Nora had. *Her daughter. I can't think of any other way to describe her.*

"We're headed out to Falling Water tomorrow. You know the Frank Lloyd Wright house built over a waterfall?" Hearing no response, she said, "I wish you were with us."

"This is Nora's time. I'd just get in the way."

"Nonsense. Why don't you come visit? Victor and I have plenty of room. We'd enjoy getting to know you."

"I can't get off work just now. Some other time, perhaps."

Changing the subject, Sarah said, "Do you have photos of Paulie you could share? I'd like to know what he looked like. He was my birth father, after all."

"He was a good-looking guy. A good father. But pictures? I never kept a family album."

"Wedding photos, maybe?"

"We didn't have that kind of wedding. It was just a family affair."

"Maybe someone took a snapshot after the ceremony or at work with some of his friends."

"I'll look, but I don't think so."

Stumped on how to continue the conversation, Sarah said. "Is there anything you'd like to ask me?"

"Like what?"

"Anything about my growing-up years? My husband? Our son?"

"I know you have a little boy. I saw that video where he interrupted you. That was sweet."

"He's quite a character. I'm sure you'll want to see for yourself someday soon."

"Hmm," she said. "I don't know when I'll be able to get away."

With nothing else to say, Sarah promised to keep in touch and said her goodbyes.

That is the strangest conversation I've ever had, she thought. *What's wrong with this woman? Why is she so passive? If I were in her position, I'd be fighting to keep the child I raised. I'd be curious about the life my birth daughter has led. I'd want to meet my grandson.*

She gripped the counter's edge as a wave of loneliness washed over her. For the first time, Sarah felt unmoored from Lilly, the woman who had raised her. But when she reached out to the woman who had given her birth, Ginny didn't grasp her hand. She was being swept out to sea.

CHERYL CALLED TUESDAY MORNING, reminding her they were scheduled to tape on Thursday. "I haven't had time to think about it," Sarah said. "Can we put it off for a week?" She was to pick up Nora in an hour and spend the day with her before they joined Lilly for dinner on Mount Washington.

"I know you're busy," Cheryl said, "but we need to release new episodes on schedule."

"Pumpernickel bread," she said. "Subscribers have requested a recipe. I've made it before, so I don't need to do extensive testing. I'll set up the time sheet and start prepping Wednesday afternoon."

Thus satisfied, Cheryl wished her luck and ended the call. As Sarah made Kellan's breakfast, she thought about all the demands on her time and expectations of others. *I wish I could just take a few days off. No Kellan, no Victor. Just me, myself, and I at a resort somewhere.*

But that was wishful thinking. After cleaning up the kitchen and kissing Victor goodbye, she dressed Kellan in his sailor's outfit, belted him into his car seat, and drove to Lilly's to collect Nora. The three made idle conversation over cups of coffee while Kellan tore around the house, pulling books out of the bookcase and scattering them around the family room.

Sarah chased after him, gathering up the volumes despite Lilly's entreaties to stop. "No, Mom, I don't want you down on your hands and knees." Despite that, Lilly leaned over to help as Nora stood by and watched.

The mess cleared up, Sarah returned her son to his carrier and snapped it into its base in the back seat. She opened the front door of her BMW to find Nora stroking the leather seat. "This is a beautiful car," she said. As Sarah pulled out of the circular drive, Nora added, "How much did it cost?"

"Too much," she said.

"What was the car you drove yesterday?"

"Also a BMW, but it's an SUV. It's Victor's car. He switched with me for the day so I wouldn't have to remove Kellan's seat." And that proved to be a mistake, she thought, recalling how the women had positioned themselves.

Two minutes later, she turned off Washington Road into a wooded residential street. "Almost there," she said.

"I didn't realize you lived so close."

Sarah glanced at her, trying to fathom whether there was a hidden meaning to the question. "I grew up here, and so did Victor. We met in high school. All our friends are here." She stopped herself from adding that their roots were so deep in this suburb that Victor had built his architectural business based on relationships and word-of-mouth.

Nora did not respond, looking around her in wonder as they passed through a grove of oak trees leading to the house. As they pulled into the driveway, she gasped. "This is yours?"

"Yes, Victor designed it and served as his own general contractor."

"It must be nice." Nora's voice dripped with envy.

"He works very hard," Sarah said, trying not to sound

apologetic. She parked in the middle stall of the three-car garage, detached Kellan's car seat from its base, and led Nora into the house through the kitchen.

Nora stood at the center island and made a complete circuit of the room with her eyes. "I've never seen a kitchen this large. In a restaurant, maybe, but not in a house."

"I cook, as you know." Kellan had fallen asleep, and she left him in his car seat while they chatted.

"But this isn't where you do your program?"

"We tape in a kitchen set downstairs. Come. I'll show you. Don't worry about him," she said as Nora eyed the sleeping toddler. "He's perfectly safe on the floor. Believe me, he'll let us know when he wakes up."

They descended the stairs to the lower level. Sarah snapped on the fixed lights so she could see the set. "It's smaller than it looks on the tube," Nora said.

"I wish I did," Sarah replied. Nora gave no sign she'd gotten the joke. "How many episodes have you watched?"

"Just two or three," she said. "I don't have time to do that kind of baking. I do, of course, but spending two days making a loaf of bread? Not me."

"Most of the time you just let the dough do its thing," Sarah said. "I can teach you."

"Where did you get the name Sal?" Nora said, ignoring the invitation.

"Mother called me Sally when I was little, but I always hated the nickname. I made her stop when I turned nine. But when I came up with the idea for this series, the resonance of the title Sourdough Sal appealed to me."

"And your husband built the set. Did he buy all this equipment?"

"I loaned myself the money." Nora's silence demanded more explanation. "I was the marketing executive with a local chain of fitness clubs when I got pregnant. Then the pandemic hit. We had to close our gyms, return client's membership fees—it was a mess. When I was ready to return to work, there was nothing left. That's why I started this business."

"I don't know why you work," she said. "If I had all your advantages, I wouldn't."Kellan let out a shout, ending what, for some reason, was an awkward moment. She took the stairs two at a time, Nora following her.

After she'd changed him, she put him in his jogging stroller and invited Nora for a walk around the neighborhood. It was a cloudless morning with the temperature in the low seventies. Feathery leaves covered overhanging branches, chickadees and goldfinch sang as they walked, and mourning doves cooed their lament. "It's beautiful here," Nora said.

"I can't imagine living anywhere else."

"But you've traveled."

"I spent the summer before college with Steve's relatives in Sweden, and a semester in London during my junior year. I saw most of Northern Europe during those four months. And you?"

"Nothing like that. In fact, I've never been outside of West Virginia until now."

Sarah was glad she'd neglected to mention she and Visitor had honeymooned in Tuscany. "Let's run for a bit." She began jogging at a slow pace but paused a minute later when she saw she'd left Nora behind. When she caught up, Sarah realized she was wheezing at the effort.

"I'm out of shape," she said.

"We can just walk. This road is a loop. If we keep going, we'll reach the house in a little more than a mile." Nora emitted a small groan. "You know all about me," Sarah said. "Tell me about yourself. You're married."

"Yes, but we're separated. Tom lost his job and went south looking for work. We haven't heard from him in months." She turned to look at Sarah. "Things are rough in coal country. Not like here. You have it nice."

She considered that for a moment. "Real nice."

"And you have a son?"

"David. He's just turned ten."

Sarah did some quick calculations. That meant she'd been eighteen when she gave birth and seventeen when she'd become pregnant. She wondered if Nora had finished high school, but she didn't know how to ask without sounding judgmental. "And your father? What was he like?"

"Paulie, you mean?" *Who else?* "He died when I was fourteen."

"He was a miner?"

"Yeah."

"What did he die of? Black lung?"

"It was some sort of accident while he was working. I don't recall much about it. One day he was there; the next day, he wasn't. Life was hard after that."

They walked in silence for nearly a minute. "I don't care to talk about it," she said. "I try not to think about it. Just put one foot in front of the other."

"All right, I understand."

They finished the loop in silence. Sarah fed Kellan, then made a shrimp salad, leaving wedges of avocado for her son.

"You got to go to college?" Nora said.

"Bryn Mawr. In the eastern part of the state," she added, seeing Nora's blank expression.

"I never got to go. With Paulie gone, there wasn't enough money."

"I'm sorry," Sarah said.

"It would've been nice. Mother says she'll make it up to me, but I don't see how."

"Ginny?" Sarah said.

"No, Lilly. She keeps telling me how sorry she is for what happened."

"You call her Mother, which is fine, but where does that leave Ginny?"

"I'm trying to figure that out," she said without hesitating. "That's what we're all doing, aren't we? Trying to figure things out?"

"Yes," Sarah said. "Yes, we are."

"You know what I should do? I should sue the clinic. They took all this away from me," she said, her voice taking on a harsh tone as she waved her arm around the dining room.

Sarah took a moment to choose her words. "Who are you going to sue after all this time? Does the clinic even exist any more?"

"No," she said. "No, it doesn't. They shut down. WVU has a big hospital in Summersville outside of Beckley, but we have nothing in Fessenden. Not a thing."

"I asked her how long she intends to stay," Sarah told Victor after she'd returned from dinner. "She waffled."

"I thought she was only staying a week."

"She's never actually said that. I think we just assumed."

"It's only been three days—two since that aunt of hers left —and you sound as if you want to be rid of her."

"It's not that." Sarah rotated her wine glass between her palms. She'd had only one glass with dinner since she was driving and felt the need for another now. "At Altius, she was all sweetness and light. She loved the ride up in the Incline, stood so long at the overlook I was afraid we would miss our reservation, and spent the entire dinner marveling at the view of the Point and the skyline beyond. She was gracious, thankful—she made all the right noises."

"But…," Victor prompted.

"When it was just the two of us this morning, she was a different person." Sarah summarized the conversation—questioning the cost of things, suggesting Sarah didn't need to work, and her obvious envy over their home. "As the day wore on, she seemed to become resentful, even petulant. Her voice and mannerisms changed. She spoke of suing the clinic where we were born, saying they took the kind of life *we* live away from her."

Victor drained his glass. "Do you want another?" he asked.

"No, I've had enough. So what do you think?"

He took his time before answering. "Try to look at it from her perspective. Two months ago, she learned she'd been switched at birth. She comes from this little coal town that she's never left, was unable to go to college, and is a single mother working in a warehouse. She comes to visit her birth family and sees us living in comparative luxury. At some level, she sees you taking her rightful place. That's not logical, but you can understand how she feels, can't you?"

Sarah stared at the lights reflected in the polished surface of the dining room table. "I suppose so."

"If you were in her shoes, wouldn't you feel the same?"

"No, because I would have gotten out of there. I would have made better life choices."

Victor picked up their glasses and took them into the kitchen. "She says Lilly is trying to make it up to her," Sarah continued as she followed him.

"How is she supposed to do that?"

"I don't know, and neither does she." She picked up a towel and dried the wine glasses he'd washed. "Or so she says."

Vincent dried his hands on a towel, observing her. "Is that what bothers you—the idea that Lilly wants to help her?"

"Don't be silly."

"Because it shouldn't matter to you. Steven and Lilly have

made it clear they still consider you their daughter. Lilly will do whatever she's going to do, and so will Nora. It has nothing to do with you. Your relationship won't change unless you make it happen."

"I hope you're right," she said, "but I have a bad feeling about all this."

~

After Cheryl's call the previous morning, Sarah had begun rebuilding her rye starter. Each loaf required a cup, which meant she needed a full quart by the time she taped. On Wednesday morning, she had enough to prepare the two loaves that she would demonstrate at the end of the episode and began building more—some for a sponge she would let rise overnight and more for her initial demonstration for the camera. It would be tight, but she felt confident she could make it.

In the afternoon, she began forming the finished loaves and discovered she'd was running low on malt syrup. Where to get at this late hour? A store in Bethel Park had long supplied every need, but they had closed during the pandemic. She recalled bringing a jar to Lilly's house months before and called her cell phone to see if she still had it.

"I'm not sure, dear," Lilly said, "but we're leaving now and will be home in fifteen minutes. Stop by, and we'll search for it in the pantry."

Sarah cleaned her hands, changed Kellan's diaper, and loaded him into his car seat. She arrived in the driveway seconds before Lilly's Mercedes pulled into the circle. Nora emerged from the passenger's side, looking radiant. Her blond hair was lighter than before; swept back in gentle waves with two ringlets on either side of her face, a recent style Sarah considered a cliché. Opening the rear door, Nora pulled out a Talbots bag.

"Hi, Noah," Kellan said.

Nora gave him a big smile. "Precocious little guy, isn't he?"

"All that and more," Sarah replied as Lilly pushed herself out from behind the steering wheel. Her hair was similarly done up, and Kellan raced to embrace her leg. As she looked at the two women, Sarah felt a stab of recognition. Their resemblance was uncanny, even given the difference in their ages. But that was only half the reason for her discomfort.

"I see you've been to the hairdresser," Sarah said.

"The spa, actually," Nora replied in her soft, sing-song voice. Holding up her hands and waving her fingers, she said, "We had manicures, pedicures, and massages. The whole works. I've never been treated so well."

Something in Sarah's expression made Lilly say, "We knew you were busy baking today."

"Still, you might have invited me," Sarah said, trying to keep her tone light. There was no mistaking the expression on Nora's face. Standing behind Lilly, she smirked.

Determined not to feed Nora's sense of triumph, Sarah said, "But I'm glad you two enjoyed yourselves."

As Lilly took Kellan by the hand, Nora said, "Can you hold this?" She thrust the package into Sarah's hand and reached into the car for a package from another fashion store in the Galleria Mall. Sarah walked toward the house without another word, hanging the Talbot's bag on the handle of the hallway closet. Nora removed it and scampered up the stairs with her treasures.

"Nora looks just like you, Mom," she said as she followed Lilly into the kitchen. "She's beautiful."

"So are you, Sarah. Don't forget that. And you don't look a thing like Ginny."

"If I lived with her, I might."

"People make their own way in this world," she sniffed.

"What are you two talking about?" Nora said. They turned to see her standing at the kitchen door.

Lilly wrung her hands, speechless, but Sarah said, "We're trying to locate a jar I left here last year." She rummaged in the pantry, moving items around until she found the container of dark liquid, a sticky surface covering the rear label. She emerged, ran the bottle under hot water, and dried it off. "I'll be off now. You two have a good evening. Say hi to Dad from both of us."

"Can you stay for dinner?" Lilly asked.

"No time," she said. Holding the container in her left hand, she scooped Kellan up in her right arm and carried him to the door. She didn't look back as she drove away, tears stinging her eyes.

～

"Can we start again?" Cheryl asked from her position before the switcher. "You're not smiling."

"Sure," Sarah said. "Sorry."

"Anytime you're ready."

Sarah took a deep breath, stared at the red light, and smiled. "There are few things more satisfying than a fresh loaf of sourdough bread." Holding up a bottle of dark porter, she added, "Particularly when you get to finish a key ingredient as a reward. I'm Sourdough Sal, and today we're going to make this delicious rye bread, just loaded with goodness."

As she always did, Cheryl asked if Sarah wanted to pause at this point and was surprised at the response.

"Yeah. Give me a minute." She leaned over the table, her head bowed as though she were thinking about what came next. "All right. I'm—shit!" Her hand brushed the beer bottle, sending its contents flying over the set and drooling onto the floor.

Both women got down on their hands and knees as Penny, Cheryl's daughter, brought a bucket and mop from the utility closet. Fifteen minutes later, having taken a fresh bottle of porter from Victor's stash, Sarah continued. "This may be the messiest dough you ever work with, so you're going to want to use your stand mixer. We're going to start with four ounces of dark beer—"

"Cut!" Cheryl shouted.

"What's the matter now?"

"Aren't you going to mention the brand name?"

"Didn't I?"

"No, you just referred to it as stand a mixer."

Sarah scratched the back of her neck as she shook her head. "Okay, let's start over."

Things continued to deteriorate. As the mixer began churning the dough—beer, malt syrup, caraway seeds, and a mix of bread and rye flour—it slowed to nearly a full stop. "I should have started with the paddle attachment," she said, interrupting her presentation. "Can we stop and begin again from that point?"

Without a word, Cheryl rolled the scene back and studied it. "We can see the dough hook in the shot as you attach the mixing bowl to the base," she said.

Sarah said nothing, peering off to the right as though distracted.

"I've got it. Clean the dough hook and reattach it. Then change to the paddle before you begin and explain why you're doing it."

"Can't you just fix it in post?" Sarah said.

Cheryl closed her eyes and leaned back in her chair. Speaking slowly, she said, "Just do it my way for once."

"All right. No need to get touchy. We'll do it *your* way."

She bumbled through the rest of the episode, mispro-
nouncing the bread as "pimpernuckel," and emitting three
damns as the gooey mess began spilling off the work surface
and, later, when the slightly risen loaf refused to drop from the
basket onto the baker's peel. At each instance, she looked
toward the camera and asked, "Can you fix it?"

Cheryl had Sarah revoice the segment where she'd mispro-
nounced the bread. She'd have to insert cover shots to mask
the edit and emit the family unfriendly words. She was silent
as she broke down the gear when at last the segment came to
an end.

"Are you okay?" Sarah asked as her partner went about her
work wearing a grim face.

"It's going to be a lot of work making this right," she said.
"But the question is, are *you* okay?"

"I have a lot on my mind."

"We both do," Cheryl said. "We *both* do."

Sarah entered her parents' house through the garage door,
calling out a cheery hello as she entered the kitchen, leaving
the loaf of pumpernickel bread on the counter. Hearing no
answer, she wandered through the lower floor. As she neared
the parlor, she heard Nora speaking quietly.

"I only brought a few dollars with me," she said. "I don't
make much at the warehouse. What little I take home goes to
support David."

Sarah clutched her hands to her mouth as though in
prayer, stepping back from the open doorway and holding her
breath as she eavesdropped.

"I understand," Lilly said. "Life hasn't been easy for you."

"I'm not one to complain." Nora's voice was saccharine,
nothing like the harsh tone she'd taken when threatening to

sue the clinic forty-eight hours before. "Still, I wish I had a bank account and could just take money out, like Sarah does."

"I'm glad to help," Lilly continued. "Let me get my purse. Steven insists I keep a hundred-dollar bill with me."

As she heard Lilly ease herself out of the wingback chair, Sarah retreated toward the kitchen.

"But I couldn't take money from you," she heard Nora call after Lilly.

Oh, I'll bet you could.

"Nonsense. I feel I owe it to you after all that's happened."

Sarah continued back-pedaling, grateful that the carpeted floor masked her footsteps. She retreated into the kitchen, opened the door to the garage, and slammed it. "Hello," she shouted.

"Oh, hello, dear," Lilly called from the living room.

"Is Nora here?"

"She's in the parlor."

But she stood in the doorway to the kitchen, her arms folded beneath her breasts, frowning. "What have you two been up to?" Sarah asked.

Lilly smiled. "Not much. We've just been visiting. Nora's telling me about her son."

There was no mistaking the snide look on Nora's face. She knew or suspected Sarah had overheard their exchange and was reveling in the fact that Lilly was dissembling. Ignoring it, Sarah said, "You must miss him."

Lilly turned, suddenly aware of Nora's presence.

"He's fine," Nora replied. "I've only been here a few days, and he's busy with his schoolwork."

"Still, I know you'll be glad to see him again. I can't stand to be away from Kellan for long."

"But you are now."

"Victor took him to the zoo. Boys' day out."

"And now it's just us girls," Lilly said. "Let me make some tea and get us a snack."

Sarah told her she'd brought fresh bread. Lilly asked how the taping had gone. Sarah responded it had been "a little rough," but said nothing more. The three sat at the kitchen table, drinking tea, ladling butter on the bread, and saying little to each other. Sarah looked from one woman to the other. She felt like an intruder. Why had she even come here? It wasn't as though she had nothing else to do.

She finished her tea and said, "I'm going home to start dinner. Mom, come walk me to the car."

Lilly followed her out the kitchen door and through the garage. As Sarah stepped aside to let her mother through the door, Nora followed behind. "Such a wonderful day," she said.

Sarah grunted her assent, hiding her annoyance that she'd been prevented from getting a private word with her mother.

"Help me identify these flowers," Nora said, locking Lilly's arm and leading her to the small garden encircled by the driveway.

"I wish you'd been here while the Lenten rose was still in bloom," Lilly said, her voice trailing off as Nora led her away. "It's not really a rose, you know...."

Sarah watched the two of them walking arm-in-arm, ignoring her. Her jaw set, she climbed into the driver's seat, started the engine, and tapped a phone number on the console's screen. When a man answered, she said, "Can you make time for me? We need to talk."

"Come in, come in." Steven stepped aside as Sarah entered his office. He closed the door after him and, instead of sitting behind his desk, dragged a chair from his round conference table and set it facing her.

"Thanks for seeing me," she said. "I know how busy you are."

"I can tell you're upset. You wouldn't have come all the way out here unless it's important." He took his hands in hers. "Are you and Victor having problems?"

"Oh, God no," she said. "Nothing like that. Everything's fine at home." Leaning back in her chair, she took a deep breath and stared at the ceiling tiles.

Her father waited, saying nothing.

"Nora is wheedling Mom for money. And she's giving it to her," Sarah continued.

Steven nodded. "How much?"

"Just a hundred dollars for now, but that won't be the end of it."

"I'm sure you're right." He rose and stared out the window, looking down at the traffic on the West Parkway. His right hand tapped a rhythmic beat on a few coins in his pocket.

"You don't seem surprised," she said.

"I'm not." He said nothing for several seconds, then, as though speaking to the glass, said,

"Your mother forms these attachments," he said, turning to face her. "You see all the direct mail solicitations we receive? It's because she contributes to everyone who writes us. She can't pass a beggar at an intersection without stopping the car and reaching into her handbag."

"That's how she got rear-ended last year."

"Yes," he said. "It would have been easier if she'd just given him the thousand bucks."

"But this is different," she said.

"Yes," he repeated, "very different."

"I can't speak to her alone, Dad. When I'm around, Nora trails her everywhere, not letting us out of her sight."

"You're kidding. No," he said, "I know you're not." He

put his hands behind his neck and slid them forward toward his chin. "She's asked me to stop by the ATM on the way home and withdraw five hundred dollars."

"But it's not just the money."

"I know. I'm not blind. I see this girl working on her."

"What are we going to do?"

"She's not getting five hundred bucks. That's for starters. As for the rest, the girl's going home on Sunday. The aunt's coming up to get her. Once she's out of sight...."

"I'm happy to drive her."

Steven chuckled. "I'm sure you are. Let us hope putting some distance between them will bring Lilly to her senses. Meanwhile, come to me with anything you see."

"I will," she said, "and thank you."

They gave each other bear hugs, and Sarah left the building, heading into the five o'clock traffic. As she crept along I-376, she recalled an incident from her college days. She and a friend had been drinking, and the friend had asked her to drive her car back to their apartment. An officer had pulled her over, and she failed a breathalyzer test. In a panic, she'd called Steven, explained the situation, and begged him not to tell Lilly.

"Who do you think you are?" he'd shouted into the phone. "I would hide nothing from your mother."

And now we're conspiring against her. He must really be concerned.

It was Sarah's turn to host Sunday dinner. She had slow cooked a pork roast while they were at church. Now she roasted small potatoes and Brussels sprouts while Victor poured wine. She placed Steven at the foot of the table, Victor at the head, Kellan between Lilly and herself on one side, and Nora and another table setting on the other.

"Who's the empty spot for?" Nora asked after they'd said the blessing.

"For Eleanor," Sarah said.

"Eleanor? What makes you think she's coming?"

"I thought she was joining us. Isn't she picking you up?"

"Oh, Dear," Lilly said, "haven't I told you?"

"No, Mother," Sarah replied, not bothering to keep the edge out of her voice. "Told me what?"

Both Steven and Victor leaned forward.

"It's the greatest news," Lilly said. "Nora's staying a bit longer."

"How much longer?" Sarah said. Victor nudged her under the table, but Sarah pulled her foot away.

"She's welcome to stay as long as she wants." There was no mistaking Lilly's icy response.

"I like it here," Nora said, speaking with her fingers again. "There's a lot more to do here than in Fessenden."

"So you're moving here," Victor said.

"Nothing like that," she said in a lighthearted voice. "But David is still in school, and I'm enjoying getting to know my family."

"Isn't that wonderful?" Lilly said.

Sarah stared at her hands, aware that Steven's steely blue eyes were fixed on her, but afraid to meet his gaze. "Very," she murmured.

Seven

SARAH KEPT to herself for three days, neither calling nor visiting Lilly. She told herself she wasn't sulking; she didn't know how to deal with Nora's sudden decision and Lilly's unrestrained enthusiasm. And she was afraid that she would say the wrong thing, driving a wedge between her mother and herself.

On Wednesday, just as she was preparing lunch, her cellphone rang. Glancing at the screen, she answered. "Hello, Mom."

"What phone do you have?" Lilly said.

"An iPhone. Why do you ask?"

"What model?"

"It's—," A warning bell sounded in her head. "What's this about?"

"Nora needs a new one."

Sarah removed her right earring, turned off the loudspeaker, and pulled the phone to her ear, all as though in slow motion. "What's wrong with her present one?"

"I don't know. Something about her carrier shutting off her signal."

"Hasn't she paid her bill?"

"It's not that," Lilly said indignantly. "It's something technical. I don't understand these things."

Sarah sighed, picturing Nora's flip phone she'd never seen her use. "They're shutting down 3G networks to make room for 5G."

"That's it. I knew you'd be able to explain it. So what model do you have?"

"An expensive one. I use it for work. She doesn't need all that. How much does she want to spend?"

Lilly's pause was almost imperceptible. "I'm buying it for her."

Closing her eyes, Sarah took a deep breath before responding. "Then she certainly doesn't need my model. Bring her here. We'll go online and find a used one. They're quite reasonable."

"I don't want to foist some old model on her. Which one do you have? Isn't it number thirteen? There are four different kinds with that number."

"Mom, where are you?"

"At the Apple store in the mall."

"Give me fifteen minutes. Then, I'll join you."

"No need. I don't want to put you out. Just tell me what model you have. That's what she wants."

"Mom, when I was growing up, you told me to be responsible for myself. You were right. I earned money for my first car; I bought my first cellphone. You taught me responsibility and self-reliance. This woman is 28, an adult. If she wants a new phone, let her buy it. I'm happy to help find a bargain for you."

"We gave you lots of help growing up." Lilly lowered her voice almost to a whisper, signaling that Nora was nearby. "She didn't have the advantages you had."

"That's not your fault, and it's not mine. She's using you. Don't you see that?"

Lilly gave a full-throated response. If Nora was nearby, she heard every word. "I want to help her, and I expect you to do the same. You sound jealous. It's unlike you."

"I'm only looking after you," Sarah said.

"I'm a responsible adult, to use your term. I can look after myself."

With that, the phone went dead. Sarah sighed and put both hands on the counter, bowing her head beneath its weight. Her body was a tree whose branches were weighed down by snow. "Don't cry, Mommy." Kellan peered up at her, his lower lip trembling.

"It's all right, Buddy. You and Daddy and I are going to look after each other. We'll be fine."

Cheryl sat at her console with Sarah alongside her as the two reviewed the edited version of the pumpernickel bread episode. In contrast to past sessions, Sarah watched the lesson without asking Cheryl to pause.

"What do you think?" Cheryl said, as the closing credits rolled.

"It seems rather choppy."

"Yes," Cheryl replied. "I had to do a lot of patchwork. It shows in places."

"The part where I change to the paddle...."

"Yes, it's awkward, but it's the best I could do with what I had."

Sarah heaved a sigh, and Cheryl braced herself for what was to come.

"Let me see the close again." Cheryl scrubbed back to the

last scene, and Sarah gazed at the screen. "There's no tease," she said.

"No, there's not."

"Did you cut it?"

"You didn't give one."

"I always preview what I'll do in the next episode," Sarah said.

"You didn't this time."

"I'm sure I did. We're doing pretzels. I'm sure I mentioned it."

Cheryl did not correct her. Instead, she opened another file, the raw video from the taping, expressing her exasperation with exaggerated clicks on the keyboard and scrubbing through the screen with vigorous swipes on the trackpad. "That's it for this lesson," Sarah's voice came through the speaker. "Be sure to give us a thumbs-up, subscribe to the series, and leave any comments you have. I respond to them all. I'm Sourdough Sal. Here's to more baking in the wild."

Sarah bit her left thumbnail. "You should have said something."

Cheryl swiveled her chair and faced her. "I had my hands full just trying to cover all the hiccups."

"Still, I wish you'd caught it."

"Sarah, I'm responsible for the technical end; you handle the content. I would have backstopped you, but this session was such a goddamn mess, I was busy covering your mistakes."

Sarah recoiled as though she'd been struck.

"You need to get it together," Cheryl said. "We were cranking these out like clockwork until a few weeks ago. Now, every session is a trial. You're missing deadlines. I sent you the proof of the recipe book over a week ago. Have you even looked at it?"

"No," she said, shaking her head as though to ward off further accusations. "I'll get to it today."

"And you haven't provided financial reports in weeks. Sarah, I haven't seen a penny from this partnership. I can't make it any longer. I have to find a steady job."

"Please don't. I need you." She reached out, grasping Cheryl's arm. "I'll loan you some money. No, I'll pay you for the time you've put in. I'll make it right. I promise."

Her frenetic response and the anxious tone of her voice startled Cheryl. "What's going on?" she asked. "You want to talk about it?"

"No," Sarah said, holding her fingertips to her temples. "It's just something I need to work out with Lilly."

"That woman is it? I thought she'd gone home."

"She hasn't and has no plans to do so. She's decided this is her home."

"And your mother?"

"She doesn't see it. Lilly doesn't realize she's being used." Raising her voice, Sarah said, "She won't even talk about it. It's as though I'm interfering when all I want is to help her avoid a mistake."

"We're never too old to stop learning the hard way. You may have to let this run its course."

"And if it doesn't?"

"Look out for yourself, not just for your sake, but for Kellan and Victor."

"Yeah," she said, nodding her head in resignation. "You're right."

Cheryl leaned over and hugged her, and Sarah wept into her shoulder. She had never felt closer to a white woman in her life. But, she told herself, I must take my advice. I must look out for number one.

～

Taking Cheryl's advice, Sarah skipped church on Sunday, reasoning that it was better if she stayed out of Lilly's way as long as Nora was around. The weather was fine, so she packed a picnic lunch while Victor mounted their kayak on the roof of his SUV. With Kellan between them, they paddled from the kayak launch around the bend to the boathouse. They went ashore, found a patch of grass the geese had not fouled, spread out a blanket, and ate a lunch of shrimp salad and deviled eggs, Kellan settling for a peanut butter sandwich.

When they'd finished, Victor ran off with Kellan to play Frisbee, which meant father floating the disk which son ran after. Sarah lay on the blanket watching them, letting the sun toast her legs and bare shoulders. This, she thought, was how life was meant to be. For a moment, she forgot about Lilly, Steven, Nora, and everyone else. This was her family; no one could separate the three of them. She would keep her distance from Lilly and Nora and try not to let their growing relationship eat at her.

Lilly, however, had other plans, calling her shortly before noon Monday. "We missed you yesterday," she said.

"We went on a picnic," Sarah replied, not hinting at her decision to give the two women a wide berth. "Victor wanted to spend time with Kellan."

"Well, you should have come to church first," Lilly said. "You should never miss Sunday service. But that isn't why I called."

Sarah waited.

"Can you come over for a few minutes? Nora's new phone arrived, and she needs help to set it up. These things are beyond me."

Sarah tried to beg off. "It's straightforward. You turn it on, answer the questions on the screen, and the phone does the rest."

"We're afraid we'll do something wrong. Please."

"All right, Mother. Let me feed Kellan, and we'll be there. I can't stay long, though."

"I know you're busy. We just need you to guide us. We don't want to lock it up or anything."

Half an hour later, Sarah pulled into the circular driveway and entered the kitchen through the door alongside the garage. Kellan ran into Lilly's outstretched arms, said hello to "Noah," and ran off searching for his grandfather, who was not at home. Sarah greeted Nora with a frosty hello, not bothering to engage her in conversation.

It made no difference. Nora launched into a replay of everything that had gone on at the service the day before—the pastor's message, the choir's anthem, and the descants the sopranos had sung over the last verse of the hymns. "They're really something," she said.

"They are," Sarah allowed. "Where's the new phone?"

Nora pointed to a small cardboard box sitting on the kitchen counter. "It just arrived this morning. I haven't opened it."

"Let's do so."

"Can you do it?" Nora asked.

"It's just the shipping container. The phone is inside in its own box." But when Nora stood by, Sarah said, "Oh, all right."

She ran a knife around the seam and opened the package. When she saw the Apple box inside, she looked up at Nora. "This isn't just the Pro; it's the Pro Max."

"Yes, isn't it great? Mom wanted me to have it."

Still, she did not open it, so Sarah did so, shaking her head at the cost, which, state and county sales tax included, approached twelve hundred dollars. "You'd think they'd provide a charger," Sarah said as she pulled the contents out of the rigid packaging, "but all you get these days is the cord."

She carried it to a side table in the den. "Dad has one of

these multi-charger blocks," she said. "There's room for a third cord, so you can plug it in here each night alongside theirs. Now for the phone. Do you know how to fire it up?"

Nora shook her head. Sarah showed her how to press the side button, and the unit came to life. Nora gasped as the logo disappeared and the first question appeared on the screen. "Accept English," Sarah said.

"Can you do it for me?"

"It's better if you learn how. I'll watch."

Lilly entered the room, smiling and holding her hands together as though in prayer.

Sarah helped Nora through each step, having her key in a six-digit passcode and helping her set up facial recognition. That done, they got to the sign-in. "Do you have an Apple ID?"

"What's that?" Nora said, using her quiet voice.

Sarah explained it to her. "You need to establish an identity. What do you want to use? There are lots of Nora's in the world. You need something unique. How about noraboras?"

Nora had her try it, and they learned it was taken. "How about nlindstrom?" Nora said.

"Hm," Sarah said, mentally rolling her eyes. She keyed it in, but that, too, had been claimed.

They settled on nlindstrom28 and moved on to establishing a password. "Choose something complex but that you can remember. Not something others could guess, like an address."

"I can't think of anything."

"One trick is to spell something backward and replace some letters with figures," Sarah prompted.

"My son's name is David. Maybe if we spelled it backward and turned the i into a 1?"

"I don't want to know your password," Sarah said. "It's something you should keep private."

But in the end, Nora insisted on getting her help, so Sarah inverted David's name, replacing the a with a 4, the i with an exclamation mark, preceding it with the month of his birth and following it with the date.

"All right, you enter it," Sarah said.

But when Nora did so, she couldn't make the password and the confirmation match, so Sarah had to do that, too. "When you get familiar with the phone, change the password. No one else should have access to it."

There was the small matter of a credit card for the account. Lilly supplied hers, which Sarah entered while keeping her reservations to herself. She looked up to see Nora smirking. They locked eyes, and the smug, self-satisfied look left her face. It was as though the curtain had dropped and Nora hadn't realized she was standing in front of it.

Sarah showed Nora how to use the mail app, had her take a few photos, and showed her where to find and edit them. Minutes later, she was exploring apps, opening and closing them as though she'd been doing it for years.

"I told you how easy it was," Sarah said to Lilly.

"Easy for you," she said.

Lilly invited her to stay for lunch, but Sarah passed, saying it was time for Kellan's nap. "Put him down in my bed."

"He sleeps better in his crib. Besides, I have work to do."

Lilly accepted the lie and thanked Sarah for taking the time. Which was more than Nora did. As Sarah bid her good-bye, the woman waved with one hand and returned to scrolling through the phone like a child with a new toy.

Sarah awoke in the middle of the night. It had happened before, so she knew why. Whenever she had too much wine with dinner—or, in this case, after dinner—she awoke once the buzz wore off. Ordinarily, she fell back asleep after a few minutes, but not now. A plan formed in her mind, one that seemed farfetched at first, but the more she thought about it now, the more she saw the possibilities.

Just as she knew why she'd awakened, Sarah knew what she would have to do before she could fall back to sleep. She rose to a sitting position and rose to her feet, careful not to wake Victor. Not that anything but a truck crashing through their dining room was likely to do so.

She poured herself a glass of ice water, grabbed a pen and yellow pad, and took her place at their breakfast nook. She drew a line down the middle of the page. At the top of the first column, she wrote pro. Atop the second, she wrote con. For ten minutes, she listed both sides of the debate. The list on the left side was longer, but the consequences on the right were more serious.

Flipping to another page, she built a decision tree. *If I say this, and she agrees, which one of us will take action? If she says no, how will I respond?* She covered most of the page with arguments and counterarguments branching out in an arc. It took her half an hour to finish, but in the end, satisfied with her work, she closed the tablet, turned off the light, and returned to bed, where she fell asleep within minutes, committed to the course of action.

～

"You're chipper this morning," Victor said as Sarah doused his Swedish pancakes in lingonberry preserves. "You were a bear last night."

Kellan chuckled, a sound that never failed to warm her heart. "Mommy's a bear."

Sarah leaned down, touched his forehead with hers, and growled. He giggled, so she did it again.

"Seriously," Victor said, "are you feeling better?"

"Very."

"And you won't tell me why?"

Should she share her plan? No, she decided. Victor was the more cautious of the two and would try to dissuade her. She knew what she wanted—what she had to do. She plated her own breakfast and sat across from him in the breakfast nook. "A new morning brings a new perspective," she said.

"And black coffee provides a clearer view than red wine."

She shrugged, ignoring the implied rebuke.

Victor asked what she had planned for the day. She told him she was taping another segment on Thursday and had to test recipes. "I'm going to pay Cheryl something to keep her going," she said. "Otherwise, I'll lose her."

"You should pay her," he said. "The woman works her—." Glancing at their son, he self-edited. "She works hard for you."

He kissed both of them, slung his backpack over his shoulder, and left for work. After cleaning up, Sarah took Kellan downstairs and sat on the floor to play with him. Then she left him to his own devices and began working on a recipe for limpa. She felt Swedish today, and the irony that she had lost the genetic link to Scandinavia didn't cross her mind.

At noon, she prepared lunch for the two of them, after which she put Kellan down for his nap. He had begun to resist this routine and even learned how to crawl out of his crib, but today she hoped he'd sleep for at least an hour, giving her time to execute her plan without interruption. As Kellan jumped up and down and talked to himself, Sarah sat on the end of their king-sized bed and read over the notes she'd made ten hours before.

She checked on him when things grew quiet in the next room. The little guy was lying on his back, his hands folded and a smile on his face. She closed the door to his room, retreated to the kitchen, took a deep breath, and dialed a number on the home phone.

"Hello?" a voice said.

"Eleanor, this is Sarah Mathews."

"I see that. We have caller ID."

"How are you?" she said.

"I'm fine. What do you want?"

So much for small talk. "Have you heard from Nora lately?"

"Of course. She calls every evening. Lilly bought her a new phone, you know."

"Yes, I helped her set it up," Sarah said, forcing herself not to match the woman's snappy tone. She glanced at her decision tree. The conversation was not going as she'd planned. She needed to seize control.

"I'm calling because I'm concerned about her," Sarah said.

She waited for Eleanor to ask why, but she said nothing. It was as though she'd anticipated what Sarah was about to say, but now that she'd broached the subject, there was nothing to do but continue.

"She's fine. That's not the problem. And she seems happy. We keep her on the go."

Again, nothing from the other end.

"But I'm concerned she's enjoying herself a bit too much."

Nora's aunt laughed, a raucous chortle, as though she'd never heard anything so funny. She ended it with a drawn-out sigh, as though exhausted with the effort.

Sarah glanced at her notes and turned them over. They offered no guidance, so she was on auto-pilot. "You think that's funny?"

"Don't you? 'Enjoying herself too much.' How is that even possible?"

"It is if it makes her ignore her home, her family, her job."

"She's taken leave from her job. She can go back whenever

she wants. As for her son, she calls David every night. He has two weeks of school left, so he's busy. He spends weekends playing with his friends. Ginny's looking after him. He's well taken care of, believe me."

"And after school's out?" Sarah said.

"Maybe he'll come visit. There's a lot more for a boy to do in Pittsburgh than here in Fessenden—museums, major league baseball, an amusement park."

"And Ginny?"

"Since when did you show any concern for her? She's the woman who gave birth to you. You haven't reached out to her. You should come visit her."

"I have my own family to look after."

"You know what's wrong?" Eleanor said. "You're not worried about Nora. You're worried about yourself. You're jealous, unable to accept the situation, angry that Lilly and Nora have established such a close bond. You feel threatened."

Sarah snorted. "Ridiculous."

Eleanor went on as though Sarah hadn't spoken. "We're all worried about you—Nora, Ginny, myself, but especially Lilly. Nora says she talks about it all the time. How angry you are. She feels she doesn't even know you anymore and feels a sense of estrangement."

Sarah closed her eyes, covered her mouth with her right hand, and held the phone away from her ear. Nevertheless, the woman went on.

"You need to get your shit together. Everyone is happy, enjoying each other's company and getting along together. But you're just dragging everyone down with your moods and resentfulness. A dark cloud hangs over that big house whenever you show up."

Sarah choked out a goodbye and ended the call. She crossed to the sink, turned on the water, and cupped her hands in it, letting it pour over her face. Her body quaked in a paroxysm of anger. And cold, naked fear.

Victor Mathews returned home in a foul mood. A client with whom he'd been working for months had decided she wanted to move the location of a full bath on the upper floor. What seemed a simple request to her was anything but, for the location she'd chosen had no plumbing leading toward it. The changes meant modifying the design from the basement through the first floor to the second. He'd tried to explain this, but she had been adamant. "Just put it between the two guest bedrooms. There's plenty of room."

This was the third major revision he had made since the client's husband had signed off on the design, and Victor wished he'd never met the couple. As he came through the door leading from the garage, he tried to put the day behind him, but when he looked at his wife, he knew worse lay ahead. Dishes were piled high in the sink, and a trail of broken crackers led through the kitchen, tracing the path Kellan had blazed during the afternoon.

And Sarah looked awful. Not that he was about to tell her that. Her hair was a mess, her "face," as she referred to her makeup, had eroded, she was still dressed in the warm-up outfit she'd been wearing when he'd left nine hours before, and he could tell she'd been crying.

"What's happened?" he said.

"I can't talk about it now. After dinner."

"You're sure? Okay. What have you chosen to fatten us up tonight?" he said, trying to keep his tone light.

"Leftovers," she said, taking a container holding the remnants of a chicken and mushroom pasta dish on the counter with a clatter and following it with a remnant of sirloin steak that had to be a week old.

"Sounds great," he said. He took the broom from the utility closet to sweep up the cracker crumbs.

"You don't have to do that," she said.

"I have to do something around here."

"You can say that again."

He knew not to respond. They ate dinner in silence, after which he put the plates and utensils in the dishwasher and cleaned the pots and containers by hand while she gave Kellan his bath. He tucked his son in and returned to the kitchen, where she'd poured herself a large glass of white wine from the refrigerator.

"So tell me," he said.

She took a sip from her wineglass and said, "Do you think Lilly is angry with me?"

Frowning, he shook his head. "Over what?"

"Does she feel estranged from me?"

"Who's the first person she called when Nora needed help with her iPhone?"

"Do you?"

Her eyes sparkled with tears. He reached out and gripped her hand. "What's this all about?"

"I called Eleanor Frangos today."

He sat back in dismay. "What for?"

"I was trying to get her help with Nora," she said. "I thought she could talk her into returning home."

Kneading his hands together, he looked away for a moment. *Why would she do that?* "I presume this did not go well."

She took him through the conversation as best she could recall it, her voice rising as she recounted the rising tension between the two. "And then she said I wasn't concerned about

Nora, but about myself. That I was jealous and selfish and that I drag everyone else down, including Lilly."

Victor slowly exhaled. "Quite a load she dumped on you."

"Is she right? Do you think Lilly really said those things about me? Said them to Nora?" Her tone took the form of a plea. She leaned forward, knitting her brows in supplication.

"Not a chance," he said.

"Do you think I'm acting selfish? That I'm jealous?"

He raised his eyes, looking at the ceiling as he searched for the right words.

"You do," she said.

"Don't put words in my mouth. I think...."

"Yes?"

He caught his breath. "I think you're taking the relationship between Lilly and Nora personally when it has nothing to do with you."

"'Nothing to do with me?'" she said, raising her voice. "It has everything to do with me."

"Try to look at this as two separate issues." Cupping his hands to his left, he said, "The first is your relationship with Steven and Lilly. Nothing's changed about that. They still treat you as their daughter, me as their son-in-law, and Kellan as their grandchild. They raised you. You have known them for over twenty-eight years. They love and respect you."

Moving his hands to the other side of the table and cupping them, he said, "The second is Lilly's relationship with Nora. Late in life, she's discovered that she gave birth to a woman she'd never met, never dreamed existed. She's getting to know her and trying to make things up to her. That's between the two of them."

"So you think I'm wrong to feel Nora is using her?"

"I don't know," he said, tossing his hands in the air. "And I don't care. Lilly bought her an expensive cell phone. So what?

She can afford it. If it makes her feel better, why should you care?"

Returning his hands to the first box he'd created, he said. "You're here, and you're solid."

"Maybe you're right."

"Compartmentalize. Keep your relationship with Lilly solid and let their relationship go wherever it will."

"You don't know how it feels," she said.

"No, I don't, but I also know that you can't change it."

His advice made sense, but how was she to do it? "I'll try," she said.

Eight

SARAH SPENT the following two days trying to put Eleanor's accusations behind her. She had plenty to do. Kellan's second birthday was the next week, and she had chosen a dinosaur theme. She sent invitations dominated by a T-Rex to seven children, three from the neighborhood and four from church, and ordered an inflatable triceratops to be installed on the front lawn.

On Thursday, she and Cheryl recorded another episode of Sourdough Sal featuring whole wheat hamburger buns. Sarah had often made these for her family, so the taping went well, save for Cheryl having to remind Sarah to smile at several points.

Sarah also gave Cheryl a check for five thousand dollars. Their project was still not profitable, but she drew on the revenue that had come in, postponing repayment for the loan she had advanced to get the series started. Cheryl thanked her, but said, "I'd still like to see a balance sheet at some point."

"Give me until the end of the second quarter," Sarah replied. "That's only five weeks from now, and it will give us a good chance to assess where we are."

"I guess that's okay," Cheryl said. "I need to decide whether we have a viable business here, and the sooner, the better."

They parted amicably, but Sarah could tell her answers hadn't satisfied her partner. The unpleasantness of the prior week still hung over their relationship.

With the Memorial Day weekend ahead of them, Victor spent Thursday evening cleaning the gas grill on the rear deck while Sarah and Kellan chased fireflies. Because the weather promised to be glorious for the weekend, Sarah considered inviting Lilly, Steven, and Nora over for a cookout after Sunday services, but she couldn't decide if she wanted them around. Despite her uncertainty over Eleanor's accusations, she had been at peace for the past three days while leaving the two women to their devices. She had not called Lilly, nor had Lilly contacted her.

That changed Friday morning when her mother called with a request. "Can you come over to help us with a technical problem?"

"I'm not a techie," Sarah said. "I rely on Cheryl for that sort of thing."

"It's a phone issue," Lilly explained. "You know your way around these things. I don't."

Sarah gave in and, fifteen minutes later, arrived at the sprawling house with Kellan in tow. "I've missed my little man," Lilly said, picking him up. "My, you're getting heavy."

Kellan squirmed to get out of her arms. "He's getting independent, too."

"He is that," Sarah said. "He has a mind of his own."

They discussed plans for the birthday party, now just five days away. "Vivian has an internship at Kraft Heinz this summer," Sarah said, "so we're putting Kellan in daycare three days a week."

"Isn't he a bit young for that?"

"It's only three hours in the morning," Sarah said, "and it will give him a chance to play with other kids."

"I'm sure you know best," Lilly said, her tone showing she thought nothing of the sort.

Sarah dismissed the rebuke. It wasn't a life sentence. "Where's Nora? And what is this phone issue?"

Lilly went to the base of the stairs and called out for the woman. "Sarah's here. She's come to fix your phone."

"Oh, all right," came the muffled reply. Nora followed a minute later, still dressed in pajamas and a bathrobe. Sarah suppressed the urge to point out it was ten in the morning. She greeted her, and Nora responded with an unenthusiastic, "Hi." But seeing Kellan, she got down on one knee and hugged him.

If asked, Sarah could not have explained why Nora's affection for her son troubled her, but it did. To end the encounter, she asked, "What's the problem?"

Lilly led her into the den, where two cellphones sat alongside each other in Steven's charging block. She picked up a brightly colored folder from beneath the table. "I've opened a checking account for Nora," she said.

"Okay," she said, drawing out her response.

"I need you to help her set up the banking thing on her phone."

"An app, you mean?" Sarah turned to Nora. "You can do that for yourself, can't you?"

"No," she said. "These things drive me nuts. Mom said you would know how to do it."

Sarah allowed herself a heavy sigh. "Give me the bank's information," she said, picking up Nora's phone.

Lilly opened the package and pulled out a printed sheet showing the account number. Sarah told Nora to unlock her phone with facial recognition, opened the app store, and clicked on the bank's mobile app. She handed the phone back to Nora. "It needs to see your face again."

"Can't you just enter my passcode? It's 987654."

"Not very original," Sarah said. "You should change that." Nevertheless, she entered it and the app installed.

Sarah helped her sign in and entered the ten-digit account number. "Now, you need to select a password," she said.

"I'll just use the same one I use for Apple."

"It should be different."

"I can't keep track of them. Just enter it."

Enter it, please, she would have told Kellan. She did as she was told, entering her son's name spelled backward with two letters replaced by digits, preceding it with his birth month and following it with his day of birth. "You need to change these passwords to something only you know," she said.

Nora ignored her. "Is that it?" Sarah asked Lilly. "Mission accomplished?"

"There's one more thing," she said. "Get into my phone and set it up so I can transfer money from my account to Nora's."

I can't believe this. She stared into her mother's blue eyes. *Yes, I can.* In a soft voice, she said, "Are you sure that's wise?"

Lilly snorted. "That's the whole point. Nora doesn't have a bank account in West Virginia. She needs to buy things on her own."

"But giving her money...," she whispered.

"How else is she to get it?" Lilly said aloud, not bothering to match Sarah's confidential tone. "She's lost her job. She doesn't have any income."

With another sigh, Sarah navigated through Lilly's phone and account passcodes without smiling. "Let's test a transfer," she said. She sent ten dollars from Lilly's account to Nora's, then picked up Nora's phone, entered her credentials, and saw the amount appear in her account. In doing so, she saw Lilly had opened the account with five hundred dollars, the amount Steven had refused to hand over. "It works," she said.

Lilly thanked her and invited her to stay for lunch ... or breakfast, in Nora's case. Sarah declined, reminding both of them about Kellan's party. She pried him away from his fire truck and led him by the hand out the kitchen door. Since Nora was still in her nightgown, Sarah sought a moment's privacy by asking Lilly to walk them to the car.

As she strapped her son into his car seat, she asked Lilly. "Are we all right?"

"What do you mean?"

"Are you angry with me?"

"Of course not. Why do you ask?"

Sarah gnawed at her lower lip, debating how much to tell her. "The word from West Virginia is that you're put out with me."

"No. Who would say such a thing?"

"Eleanor. I won't go into details, but she claims you feel our relationship is strained."

"Nonsense. That woman!"

"I wonder where she got it," Sarah said, nodding toward the house.

"Are you accusing Nora of telling tales like that?" Her tone conveyed an unmistakable rebuke.

"Eleanor conveyed enough background to tell me she was getting information from somewhere."

"Well, Nora wouldn't do that. She loves you."

Yeah, yeah, yeah, Sarah thought. "All right, Mom. As for the money, I hope you know what you're doing. I have your best interests at heart."

"I hope so," Lilly said. With that, she turned and walked away.

~

On Saturday morning, Victor joined Steven and two of his Eagle Energy colleagues for a round of golf at St. Clair Country Club. Victor wasn't a member there. He couldn't afford the entry fee and, even if he had, wouldn't have justified it based on his low level of interest in the game. Golf was Steven's passion and St. Clair his domain, so much so that even on Memorial Day weekend, he had snared an eight o'clock tee-off time. It was an overcast, muggy morning, and the foursome were grateful for the early start.

Victor was along for the ride, his purpose for joining his father-in-law having nothing to do with chasing white balls over green fields. He was happy to hack out a six-over-par, the best he'd ever played at the course. "You're coming along," Steven said, giving him a playful punch to the shoulder as they signed their cards.

"I'll never match you," Victor replied. "I don't have the time to play." Or the enthusiasm, something he'd never admit to Steven since it would take him down a notch in the man's estimation.

After changing out of clothes wet with perspiration, they entered the Terrace Lounge with its sweeping view of the course and ordered late lunches and drinks. Steven and his companions ordered steaks. Victor, who was cooking out that night, stuck with a burger and beer.

The men bantered about sports—prospects for the Steelers' upcoming season which, with Ben Roethlisberger having retired, they judged poor; those for the Pirates, less so, as they operated almost as a farm club for richer teams.

After lunch, Steven's co-workers peeled away while Steven and Victor remained. "What's on your mind?" Steven asked. "You rarely ask to join me." He stared at Victor while the younger man searched for words.

"This is about Nora, isn't it?" Steven said when Victor balked.

"That and more," the younger man said. "How closely are you following this relationship?"

Steven gave a wry smile. "As much as I'm forced to." Noting Victor's confused look, he said, "I urged Lilly to proceed cautiously. As you can see, she's gone all in. I'm sure your concern is how Sarah is taking it. Does she feel threatened?"

Victor stroked his chin as he considered how much to say. He did not want to betray his wife's confidence. "Nora thinks up ways to exclude her."

"Hmm," Steven said. His blue eyes, usually alert, clouded over. "I was afraid of something like this," he said, concealing the fact that Sarah had told him as much. "It's one reason I told Lilly to take things slow."

Assuming responsibility for what Sarah had told him, Victor said, "Nora is Janus-like. In front of Lilly, she's all sweetness and light. When she's alone with us, though, we see another side of her—challenging, contentious...."

"I haven't witnessed that. I'm not disputing you. She just doesn't act that way in front of me. But, of course," he said, "she wouldn't."

"If it's not too personal a question, how do you feel about her? She is your daughter."

"Technically." Steven looked out the long window of the lounge toward the rolling, manicured lawn. He frowned as he studied the landscape and signaled for another round of drinks. "She was raised in coal country by a mining family. I don't want to sound like a snob, but that's a different culture than ours."

"It's honest work," Victor said.

"It is," he admitted. "You're designing high-end homes. Is that what you set out to do when you went to college?"

Victor blinked at the abrupt change in subject. "No, you know that. I thought I wanted to go into medicine."

"Into medical research, as I recall, but you found advanced chemistry wasn't your thing. And after drifting for a semester, you decided to study architecture, which required a transfer from Pitt to CMU." Victor nodded in agreement. "Designing suburban houses—was that your dream?"

"No, I wanted to design office buildings—high rises. But no firm would take me on. I don't know if the economy was at fault, there was a glut of architects doing the same thing, or I just didn't have what they needed."

Steven pointed a long, bony finger at him. "So you adapted. From medicine to architecture, from office complexes to McMansions. You adapted, and you prospered. That's the cultural difference I'm talking about. West Virginia is full of people who were miners because their fathers were miners because their fathers were miners. It's all they know. They say mining is in their blood, but mining is changing, and they won't. That's why drugs are such a problem down there."

He spoke as if West Virginia were thousands, rather than dozens of miles from where they were sitting. Though tempted to point out that his parents' means had enabled him to make choices, Victor let it pass. He wasn't there to debate Steven, but to persuade him to get involved.

The server brought Steven a gin and tonic and Victor a beer he didn't want, but the liquor loosened the man's tongue. It was often hard to tell what lay behind those steel-blue eyes, but not today.

"So what concerns you about Nora...," Victor prompted.

"Nurture over nature, to turn the phrase around. She may be our daughter genetically, but from what I've seen, that's all she is. So what is she doing here?"

"Are you aware Lilly has opened a bank account for her?"

"Are you sure?" Steven asked. "Of course you are. And I suppose she's putting money in it. How much?"

"Five hundred that we know about."

"Shit!" He drained his glass in one gulp. "I thought I'd put a stop to that."

"So," Victor said, staring at his beer, unwilling to make eye contact, "what are we going to do about it?"

"Do?" He made a guttural sound that might have stood for I-don't-know. "Lilly is enjoying this. Unless it gets out of hand, I can't get involved."

Why the hell not? Victor stared at the man, willing him to explain himself. Instead, Steven said, "Is there anything I can do for Sarah?"

Victor shook his head, defeated. "Just be there for her. She's daddy's girl. Always has been. Always will be."

"You're her husband," Steven replied, pointing an accusing finger at him. "Let her know she's loved."

"I do, and I will."

"If that's not enough," Steven said through a long sigh, "send her to me. Not that she'll need your encouragement. She never has."

With that, he signed for the check and rose from the table, their meeting at an end. Victor walked him out, concerned more for the man's three shots of hard liquor than his light beers.

He drove home slowly, hoping that Sarah wouldn't find out about their conversation. She would be annoyed with both of them.

After a humid weekend, Memorial Day brought temperatures soaring close to ninety, the hottest day of the year so far, and a record for the month. At this rate, it promised to be a scorching summer. As they sat at the breakfast nook, Victor said, "Let's take off for the day."

"Agreed," Sarah said. "We need a break."

Half an hour later, with Sarah having packed a picnic lunch, they piled into Victor's SUV and headed south on Route 43 toward Uniontown, then east to Ohiopyle. Victor donned his child carrier, knelt as Sarah strapped Kellan in, and the three set off along the Laurel Highlands Trail. They hiked for two miles, returned to their car, and headed into town.

Sarah had prepared chicken salad sandwiches, fruit, and macaroni salad. They sat on the rocks along the Youghiogheny River as they ate, Kellan devouring the pasta salad as though it was his last meal. A train crossed the railroad bridge, and the toddler jumped up and down, shouting, "Look, Daddy!"

Their lunch finished, they continued down the river walk and stood at the overlook above the rapids, Victor clasping Sarah as he wrapped his arms around her. Left to his own devices, Kellan approached the vertical bars around the overlook and stuck a leg through.

"Kellan, no!" Sarah broke from Victor's grasp and pulled her son to safety.

"There's no way he could have gotten through them," Victor said. "They're spaced close together."

Clutching Kellan's hand, she turned on him. "You don't understand what he's capable of. We have to watch his every move."

"All right," he said. "Sorry."

They returned to the car, Kellan between them, swinging him in the air twice as they walked. "I'm sorry for yelling at you," she said as Victor secured the boy in his car seat. "This thing with Nora has me on edge."

"I know," he said, patting her on the knee. "But you're right. I need to pay closer attention." He turned on the engine. "Do you still want to go to the park, or shall we bag it?"

"Whatever you want."

"Let's not let her ruin this day," he said, backing out of his parking space. "We're here. Let's show Kellan the falls."

Ten minutes later, they entered Ohiopyle State Park. The parking lot was packed this holiday afternoon. Victor dropped Sarah and Kellan off and parked along Kentuck Road, hiking back to join them. They strapped their son into his carrier and took the staircase down to the top of Cucumber Falls, pausing at the observation area for a few minutes before continuing to the base.

The thirty-foot cascade created a light spray, and as the cool mist enveloped them, Kellan giggled. "This is a waterfall," Victor said.

Kellan giggled again and tried to mimic the word.

"This is the most beautiful spot in Pennsylvania," Sarah said. "We're lucky to have it almost in our backyard."

"And we're fortunate to have each other," Victor said. He wrapped his arm around her, and she returned the gesture.

From behind him, Victor heard a small voice say, "I love you."

"We love you, too, Buddy," he said, as Sarah leaned over and kissed the boy.

Returning up the staircase, they exited the parking lot and walked to the car. As Victor knelt, Sarah said, "Our little man has fallen asleep." She unstrapped him from the carrier, and Victor secured him in his car seat.

"Since he's out," he said, "let's take in one more thing." He drove south on Sugarloaf Road until he reached a turnoff at Baumann Rock Overlook. "You go," he said. "I'll stay with Kellan."

Sarah walked the length of a football field until she reached the overlook of the deepest canyon in the state. Unlike those of the West she'd visited as a child, the vista below her was not red rock, but green foliage—mile upon mile of tree-covered hills and valleys stretching so far that the verdant hews turned blue, almost blending into the horizon.

A sob caught in her throat, and she didn't know why. It

had been such a wonderful day. Was she mourning what she felt she was losing, upset over the unraveling of her relationship with Cheryl, or dreading tomorrow's return to reality? She couldn't say. All she knew was that, despite being surrounded by all this beauty and the love of her family, she was drowning in depression.

She dried her tears on a crumpled bit of tissue paper, walked back to the car, and traded places with her husband, who appeared not to notice her red eyes. Kellan slept all the way back to Upper St. Clair, awakening only as they pulled into their driveway. "Thanks," she told Victor as he led Kellan into the house. "This has been a perfect day."

Once inside the house, however, her gloom returned for, picking up the phone she had chosen to leave behind for the day, she found an email message from Cheryl: "I need an accounting of our funds. Please provide it by noon tomorrow."

She had to prepare dinner, and the following day was consumed with putting together Kellan's party. She opened a reply and dictated it into her phone, hoping some of her anger would come through: "I am swamped tomorrow and will provide a statement at the end of June, as we agreed."

Sarah read it over and hit send.

Cheryl arrived early for her appointment with attorney Theresa Simon. Two o'clock came and went as she fidgeted in the second-floor waiting room on Greentree Road near the entrance to Parkway West. The room was sparsely furnished. Three single chairs and one padded bench surrounded a table containing legal magazines and brochures for the practice. A large print of what appeared to be an Italian coastal village adorned the wall above the bench, the only splash of color in the room apart from a pair of potted palms that looked in need of care.

The drab surroundings made her wonder whether she'd picked the right law firm. As she sat there doubting, she questioned whether it was best to consult an attorney, for once she set things in motion, there would be no turning back.

As she was gathering her notes and shoving them into her backpack, a woman opened the doorway to the left of the window. "Ms. Price?" she said, extending her hand. "I'm Theresa Simon."

She was shapeless, slender to the point of emaciation, with close-cropped gray hair and craggy features that ended in a pointed chin. "I apologize for keeping you waiting," she said. "I have to file a motion before the circuit court today and had to make some last-minute changes."

Concealing her annoyance, Cheryl assured her she understood. The attorney led her along a hallway that passed two small conference rooms and a suite of offices. The attorney's office was at the far end of the corridor, near a door that Cheryl assumed led to an emergency stairway. Law books lined a floor-to-ceiling bookcase against the far wall. Before it was a desk containing a computer, a notepad, a small container of pens and pencils, but no file folders. The attorney directed her to a small round table against a wall that held photos of children of various ages and shots of a middle-aged man and woman, a younger version of the lawyer, taken at locations throughout the world, from the Eiffel Tower to what looked like a Japanese palace.

"What can I do for you?" Ms. Simon said as Cheryl took the offered chair.

Cheryl held her notes in shaking hands. "I'm not sure you can. I don't know if I should even be here."

"Why don't you tell me your problem and we'll decide together?"

Taking a deep breath and pulling her black curls behind her ears, Cheryl recounted the last two years of her life, beginning with her first meeting Sarah during work her agency had done for Sarah at the fitness club, losing her job during the pandemic, her partnership in Sourdough Sal, Sarah's current preoccupation with a family matter, and her failure to provide the accounting she'd been requesting. "And when she put me off last night," she concluded, "I called you."

The attorney, who had made notes through the narrative, said, "May I see a copy of your agreement?"

Cheryl gulped. "I don't have one."

"You've lost it?"

"No, there is none," Cheryl said. "We've done all this on a handshake and a smile."

The attorney's sigh conveyed displeasure.

"I guess that wasn't a good idea," Cheryl said. "Am I just out what's owed me?"

"Not necessarily. What is your understanding with her?"

"We're to split everything fifty-fifty."

"And what is everything?" Simon asked.

"Advertising revenue from YouTube, profits from the book, although she has yet to sign off on the final draft, and revenue from product endorsements."

"And she handles the money? Is it held in a separate account?"

"I don't know," Cheryl said, her voice cracking as she realized how little she knew about the arrangement.

"And you've made what out of this 'partnership?'" the attorney said, her voice conveying her contempt for the term.

"She gave me a personal check for $5,000 last week."

"Drawn on her own account? Do you have it with you?" She held out her hand.

"No, I... cashed it," Cheryl said in a halting voice. "Was that wrong?"

"It complicates matters." She leaned back in her chair in thought, tapping her pencil. "I'm tempted to draw up a letter of agreement covering the partnership and have her sign it."

"I'd like that," Cheryl said.

The attorney continued to think. "But on second thought," she said, "she might simply deny its terms and say you misunderstand them. I don't suppose anyone has witnessed this conversation?" Cheryl shook her head. "Then we're going to issue a demand letter for an accounting of all revenue and expenses."

"Isn't that what I sent her by email on Monday?" Cheryl asked.

"You did, but this is a formal notice stating precisely what we want, when we want it, and what happens if we don't get it."

"That being?"

"The letter will state that it's to avoid further legal action. It's an 'or-else' without stating what that might mean. You're not threatening her." Simon leaned forward as if to reassure her. "You're telling her what she needs to do to avoid threats. She sounds like a smart lady. She'll know what it means."

Cheryl nodded. "And what should I do in the meantime?"

"Nothing. Do no more work for her; don't contact her."

"Her son has a birthday party tomorrow."

"Send your regrets."

"I've bought him a birthday present. I don't want him to suffer for his mother's actions."

The attorney leaned forward, placing both fists on the table. "I can only advise you. She won't get the letter for several days. Attend if you feel you must, but avoid any discussion of business matters. If she tries to draw you in, just tell her you can't discuss it now. It's a child's party. There should be enough confusion to give you an out. All right?"

"Okay," Cheryl said, taking the extended hand and rising.

The attorney escorted her back to the waiting room. Cheryl returned to her car on wobbly legs, regretting the need to take action, but feeling sure that Sarah had taken advantage of her.

~

June 3 dawned sunny and cloudless, and Sarah beamed as she prepared breakfast for her family. "Happy birthday, Buddy," Victor said as he entered the kitchen, tousling Kellan's hair as he did every morning. He hugged Sarah as she flipped the pancakes and poured himself a cup of coffee. "What time do these miscreants arrive?"

"Noon," Sarah said. "I thought I told you that."

"I'm sure you did. I have to meet a client at nine, but I'll be back in plenty of time."

"Must you?" She turned with the spatula in her hand. "I need you to pick up the dinosaur plates and party hats."

"Taken care of." He placed a pancake before Kellan, who picked it up and began gnawing around the edges. "They're in the car."

"And you promised to hang those plastic velociraptors on the ceiling of the downstairs playroom. I have to roll out the pizza dough and finish decorating the cake." Sarah had baked a multi-tiered cake the day before and shaped it into an egg, with a protrusion on one side that would become the eye of a baby brontosaurus emerging from its shell.

"I'll take care of it as soon as I finish breakfast. Why don't you let me pick up the pizza so you have one less thing to worry about?"

"I bake," she said, fixing him with a look that might have said, Who do you think you're talking to? "The other mothers will expect my pizza."

They finished breakfast. Victor stood on a ladder,

threaded the party decorations through the ceiling tile grids, and left.

After cleaning up the kitchen, Sarah surrounded Kellan with toys on the dining room floor where she could monitor him, removed the pizza dough from the refrigerator and cut it into four pieces she formed into balls, and finished decorating the cake. It was, she thought, a thing of beauty, light green icing with blue splotches, darker green for the figure of the emerging brontosaurus, white highlights, and jelly beans forming the eye.

True to his word, Victor arrived home at ten-thirty. He inflated the triceratops and, just in case any parent would miss the ten-foot monster in the front yard, filled balloons with helium and tied them to the mailbox post. He changed Kellan's diaper and dressed him in a blue sailor's suit Sarah had bought for the occasion.

"I don't know what I'd do without you," Sarah said when he returned.

"Have a less ornate party," he shot back. "Why don't you dress while I roll out the dough?"

Sarah hesitated. "Are you sure you know how?"

Without another word, he rolled out a round of dough, picked it up, and began spinning it in his hand, moving his arm up and down as it spread itself in all directions. "I didn't know you could do that," Sarah said.

"Before I met you, I had to fend for myself. I still remember a thing or two."

At 11:50, the thundering herd began arriving. Eight children kicked balls around the yard and crashed into the towering triceratops, screaming their lungs out while their mothers sipped mimosas Victor prepared.

Cheryl arrived shortly before noon and offered to help in the kitchen. "I think I have things under control," Sarah said, then edited her response. "Why don't you paint the tomato sauce onto the dough while I add the cheese?"

"Where's your mother?" Cheryl asked, as she began working.

"She and Nora should be along soon. They had to pick up something at Target."

"Nora? I actually get to meet this woman?"

"Lucky you," Sarah said as she fed the first pie into the pizza oven.

Ten minutes later, Lilly and Steven arrived. Nora trailed behind them, carrying a wrapped box about eighteen inches in length and a foot high. She placed it on the table of presents at the end of the outdoor picnic table and joined Victor and Kellan's grandparents as they watched the children play. Cheryl left to join them, and as Sarah watched through the kitchen window, Lilly handled the introductions.

Sarah took the second pizza from the oven and replaced it with the third. Calling on Victor to help, they carried the two finished pizzas outside. "Come on, kids," she called. "Lunch is served." She served the pizzas on paper plates while Victor poured lemonade for both children and adults.

Moving back and forth between the patio and the kitchen, Sarah caught only snatches of the conversation between Nora and Cheryl. Their discussion, animated by Nora's delicate hand gestures, ceased whenever she approached. Before paranoia overtook her, Sarah realized it was Nora who was interrupting the flow. Once again, Lilly took no notice of Nora's mind games.

Victor cleared the table, dumping the paper plates and plastic cups into a large garbage bag. He sat Kellan in the middle of the bench, ready to open his presents. Before Sarah could stop her, Nora took a seat alongside him and began cooing at him. "Look at all these presents," she said as Sarah and Victor moved them to the table.

Nora handed him the first present, and Kellan tore at the wrapping paper. Since a few children came from families who were not well off, Sarah's invitation stipulated that no one should spend more than $30 on a gift. Almost all presents had a dinosaur theme, and as he opened each one, Nora asked him to tell "Auntie Nora" what it was.

"A brontosaurus," he told her, his brown eyes looking up at her with unrestrained affection.

"Isn't he brilliant?" she said to the parents surrounding the table.

Shielding her mouth with her hand, Sarah turned to Victor. "What's she doing?" she said. "Who does she think she is?"

Victor sighed and shook his head, but offered no other support. She wanted to intervene—wanted Victor to do so—but she couldn't see a way to do so. Nora had planted herself next to her child and taken over.

"Thank Jenny for the nice present," Nora prompted.

"I've taught him to thank everyone," Sarah snapped. "Give him a chance."

Nora flashed a cunning smile, sweeping her eyes across the sea of mothers as if to suggest she was humoring her while Sarah seethed.

And she had coached him well. Kellan only needed two reminders to thank gift-givers. As it was, he was overwhelmed, wanting to play with each item before opening the next. It was a far cry from his first birthday, Sarah recalled, when the unaccustomed excitement had produced tears of frustration.

With the children's presents out of the way, Steven went to his car and returned with a pint-sized tricycle. Victor unveiled a toy train set. Cheryl had brought along a plastic tool set.

"I'm saving the best for last," Nora said. Reaching behind

her, she placed the large box in front of him. "Look at what Auntie Nora bought you."

She helped Kellan remove the wrapping paper, revealing a box whose artwork resembled a dinosaur's head. She opened the box and extracted the item. "It's an electronic mask in the shape of a velociraptor. It lights up and makes noises." She pushed a button, and the head let out a mighty roar. "You wear it."

She attempted to place it over Kellan's head, but he squirmed away.

"He's frightened by it," Sarah said.

"He just needs to get used to it."

She pushed it down over his head, but Kellan bolted from the table, shouting, "No. Don't want to."

"Please stop," Sarah said. "You're scaring him."

Swinging her legs across the bench, Nora said, "He'll love it when he sees what it does." She approached the child, still carrying the mask in her hands. Kellan recoiled in a corner of the patio, and Sarah blocked her path.

"Leave him alone," she said.

"I spent good money on this," Nora cried, dropping her sing-song tone.

"It's not your money," Sarah matched Nora's volume, but her tone was low and menacing rather than shrill. Alerted by the disagreement, two parents stopped their conversation and looked at the pair in shocked silence.

Nora drew herself to her full height, looking down on her. "How dare you?" she said.

"It's mother's money. You're making a big splash, trying to outdo everyone. This isn't even age appropriate."

"What does that even mean?"

"It's for a six-year-old or older," Sarah said, wielding the empty box as though it were a weapon.

"Stop it!" Lilly stood off to the side, tears cascading down her cheeks. "Both of you, stop it now!" Both women turned and looked at her. "Sarah, I can't believe you're being so hurtful. Nora's done nothing wrong. She spent hours searching for something she thought Kellan would like."

Sarah stared at her mother in disbelief. "She was attacking Kellan. She scared the hell out of him."

A mother grabbed her son by his hand and began making her way to her car. As though on cue, others rounded up their children.

"Mother—"

"You ruined this party," Lilly said. "What a terrible thing to do." She turned on her heels, motioning Steven to follow her. But Nora was not about to leave without getting in the last word.

Towering over Sarah, whose fists were clenched and head bowed, she hissed, "I wanted to buy Kellan a birthday present, but I have no money. Yes, Mother helped me." Her eyes watered as she said, "You have no idea what it's like. I deserve anything she gives me." She turned without another word, leaving Sarah stunned, mortified, and feeling terribly alone.

Nine

SARAH AWOKE the following morning feeling like she had used a hair dryer on her eyes and tongue. She sat up in bed and leaned to her right, uncertain where up was. "Good God." It was more a moan than a statement.

Hearing her, Victor came to the bedroom door, leaning against the jam with his arms folded. "Ready to face the world, are we?"

"No," she said, "and don't make fun of me."

"I'm not." He moved closer and sat at the foot of the bed. "What can I get you?"

"What time is it?"

"After nine."

"I have to get Kellan—"

"To daycare. I took care of it. Can I make you something? Scrambled eggs? Toast?" When she didn't reply, he added, "Broiled lamb kidneys?"

"Just coffee," she said. She lowered her legs to the floor and wobbled toward the kitchen. Victor offered his arm, and she took it. He added milk to the dispenser and started the espresso maker, something else she'd received from a manufacturer who wanted her to tout it. He poured foam over the double shot, and she thanked him with a half-smile and nod.

"How bad was I?" she asked.

"You weren't bad," he said, accentuating the final word. "Just loud. You went on and on about Nora and Lilly, repeating the same thing—that she'd attacked Kellan. Which was true. I said that the first six times you mentioned it and then realized you weren't listening."

"What else did I say?"

He paused and reached out for her free hand. "You mentioned you always knew something was wrong and never felt like you belonged."

"I said that?"

"More than once."

"It's true," she said as tears coursed down her cheeks. "I don't look like them. I don't have the same interests. During that summer in Sweden, I kept looking at all their trim bodies, fair skin, and blonde hair. I sensed I wasn't a part of them, that I was an intruder."

"Oh, God, Sarah. You do belong. You belong to Kellan and to me, and we belong to you. We're a family. And guess what? Steven and Lilly belong to all of us. Just keep that in mind, and you'll see."

She sniffled into a tissue. "Thanks," she said. "You're right. I have both of you. We are a family. But Lilly? I'm not so sure I'll ever feel the same toward her, nor she to me. Something..." She squinted and held up a close fist. "Something ripped apart yesterday. I don't think we can mend it."

"She'll get over it. You both will."

"So for the moment," she said, as though he hadn't spoken, "I'm doing nothing. I'm not calling. Not visiting. No more early morning bread delivery. She'll just have to work out this Nora thing on her own. This is my family, and I'm devoting full time to both of you."

~

Sarah arrived at Cheryl's Brookline home wearing a smile and carrying a large manila envelope. Cheryl stepped back when she entered, awaiting an explosion, but everything in Sarah's demeanor suggested she had not yet received the demand letter from her attorney.

"God, it's hot today," Sarah said. "Do you have the AC on?"

Cheryl lowered her eyes. *Why not be upfront about it?* "I can't afford it," she said.

"Yeah, the rates are going through the roof. Everything is." Sarah gave no sign she had grasped the implications of what her partner had told her.

"Can I get you something? A Coke? Iced tea?"

"No need. I have to pick up Kellan by noon, so I can't stay. But I have something for you," she continued as she thrust the envelope into Cheryl's hands. "I've finished the book."

"Oh," Cheryl said. "Okay."

"What's the matter? You don't seem pleased. I know it's taken me too long, and I'm sorry. But I spent the weekend reviewing the edits, and it's finished."

"No," Cheryl said, "that's great." She sat at her dining room table and emptied the contents of the envelope on the table. Paging through it, she glanced at Sarah as she paced back and forth in a blue mini dress with its butterfly print. Over two hundred dollars, she guessed, and a bit too flouncy on a woman who could stand to lose a few pounds. And here she was in a pair of jeans and a sleeveless tank top, sweltering through the warmest day this year.

Cheryl stopped herself; she was being petty. She turned a few more pages, studying the few corrections. It shouldn't have taken so long. But this was good. It was a book she would have bought for herself if she'd chanced upon it.

Which gave her the thought. If Sarah hadn't received the letter, perhaps Theresa Simon had yet to send it. And if she could solve the problem herself...

"I'll make the changes to the layout this afternoon and send them off to the printer," she said. "And now that it's finished, can we have a little business discussion?"

Sarah sat across from her and folded her hands on the table. "Of course. What's on your mind?"

"How many months have we worked together?"

"Since last fall. Eight months now."

"Don't you think it's time we had a written agreement?"

"As to...?" Sarah said.

"Everything. The terms of the partnership, mutual responsibilities. revenue split and reporting schedule, how funds are handled...." Cheryl trailed off, trying to recall all the items the attorney had mentioned.

Sarah frowned. "I thought we understood all that."

"But there's nothing in writing. We have a YouTube show that's growing with each episode. We have endorsements and are about to publish a cookbook. It's getting to be a big deal." She recognized she was pleading.

Sarah let out a prolonged sigh, then shrugged. "I suppose you're right. We've been running this by the seat of our pants. It's time we got serious."

"Thank you," Cheryl said, kicking herself for groveling.

"I'll have my attorney draw something up. It shouldn't cost us much. It's pretty straightforward."

She rose to leave, and Cheryl didn't keep her. She had to head Theresa Simon off before she mailed that letter.

Kellan was finishing his lunch, babbling about playground activities at daycare, when the doorbell rang. Sarah answered it to find Dave, the postman, standing at the door. "Registered letter for you, Mizz Matthews," he said. "You'll have to sign the green card."

"For my husband," she said as a statement rather than a question.

"No, it's addressed to you."

"Thanks," she said, "I think."

Dave laughed and tossed a wave over his shoulder as he returned to the right-hand drive Jeep. Sarah closed the door, staring at the return address: Gabriel, Larkin, Milewski, and Simon. A law firm, but one she'd never heard of. What could they want with her?

She slit the letter open with a steak knife, scanned it, then studied it. Cheryl was demanding a full accounting within ten days. The envelope also enclosed a draft partnership agreement.

How could she? Not three hours before, Cheryl had asked for an agreement, never mentioning that she'd set the wheels in motion herself. And with this rude demand.

"You've betrayed me," she said aloud.

~

As soon as she received the letter from Cheryl's attorney, Sarah made an appointment to see her own lawyer. Victor used William Cartwright for his business agreements. The lawyer had set up an estate plan for Victor and herself, advising that "it's never too soon."

After he read the demand letter, he asked who had witnessed her verbal agreement with Cheryl.

"No one," she said. "Victor knows the details but wasn't involved in the discussions."

"So it's your word against hers."

"Yes, but... I'm not contesting our agreement. Cheryl and I are equal partners. We're in this together."

"Will you be after, as you put it, she's blindsided you?"

"I hope so. I'm nothing without her. And," she said, raising her voice, "I don't want to get into a legal battle. That's not why I'm here. I need to know how to respond to this."

Peering over his half-frame reading glasses, he posed a series of questions. As he drew her out, she realized Cheryl had a point. She didn't know their financial condition and had nothing in writing to protect herself.

"Is there anything in the accounts you're afraid to show her?" the lawyer asked.

Sarah shook her head. "Everything's as it should be."

"Then I advise you to do as she asks," he said. He recommended she hire a CPA to review the financials and that she establish a separate account for revenue and expenses. "Once you've done so, I'll file our response. As to the partnership agreement, there are elements of this draft that need to be changed. Let me prepare our own version and present it as a counter-proposal."

He pointed out a few elements of Theresa Simon's draft that seemed innocuous to her. She suspected he was just padding his bill, but he wore her down. "I want this done expeditiously," she said. "I don't want it hanging over us." Sarah knew that until they resolved their issues, Cheryl would spend no more time on the book, and they would record no new episodes.

"I'll let her know this is coming," she said.

"No, let us handle this attorney-to-attorney."

"But I need to tell her something. I can't just leave her in limbo."

"I'll have my secretary call Ms. Simon and advise her we're responding. She was a student of mine at Duquesne."

Sarah left, feeling more apprehensive than when she'd arrived.

~

Sarah spent the next two days meeting with Victor's CPA. She took Sarah's spreadsheet, tallied it with receipts, and by Friday had a statement ready for Cartwright to transmit to Cheryl's lawyer. Throughout the week, her discomfort grew. Cheryl had demanded something of her, and she hadn't responded. Why, she wondered, hadn't she just done what Cheryl asked of her in the first place?

This flurry of activity kept her from reaching out to Lilly. This was just as well, as she'd promised Victor she would keep her distance. On Friday, Victor proposed a weekend at Presque Isle on Lake Erie, giving the two of them a needed rest and Kellan a chance to play in the sand.

She didn't speak to her mother until ten days after the birthday party had ended in a screaming match, and it was Lilly who broke the silence. Sarah had spent the morning helping at the day care center and returned home to find a voicemail message on her cell phone: *Call me when you have the time.*

She returned the call, but when she got no answer, called Lilly on her home phone. "Where've you been?" Lilly said. "I haven't heard from you in days."

"Busy, Mother. Work issues."

"I hope there's nothing wrong."

"It's all being worked out. There's nothing to worry about."

"But you could have called," Lilly said.

Sarah considered whether to confront her before speaking, then edited her response. "The last time we spoke, I had the impression you were angry with me." Which was putting it mildly.

"I wasn't angry. I just didn't care for the way you treated Nora."

"How about the way Nora was treating Kellan? You don't force a child to do something he doesn't want to, especially when it disturbs him. I was right to call her on it."

"She was just trying to show him how his present worked."

Sarah ignored her. "Nora didn't buy that present. You did. Whether you paid for it yourself or gave her the money for it, she spent your money to make herself look good."

"That's not why I bought him a present!"

Sarah pulled the phone away from her ear as the woman's voice erupted at full volume. "Nora," she said, "why are you on this call?"

"Because you're talking about me, that's why."

"I was talking to *my mother*. This is a private conversation between the two of us. I didn't know you were lurking in the background."

"I'm not lurking. Mother knows I'm here."

"Is that true?" Sarah said.

"Well, I..." Lilly let her response hang in midair. *Not true,* Sarah thought. *Lilly had no idea Nora was eavesdropping.*

"I am ending this call," Sarah said. "Mother, you need to think about what's just happened. You and I will continue this conversation when we're alone."

She hung up without waiting for a response. Her heart raced. She clutched her iPhone so hard her hand hurt.

But that was not the only source of her pain.

～

Sarah prepared Kellan's lunch in silence. Rather than his usual rambunctious self, he sat quietly, his eyes following her as she moved about the kitchen. Sensing his apprehension, she said, "It's okay, Buddy. Everything will work itself out."

He returned her smile, but his continued reticence showed he felt the tension his mother was undergoing. So when she suggested a nap, he crawled out of his high chair and headed to his room, rather than fighting the notion as he had begun to do.

After checking on him, she sat at the kitchen table, drawing endless circles on a notepad as her thoughts churned. She had to take action, but what?

As she considered her options, an idea took shape. On one level, it made sense, but the course she was contemplating was risky. As she invariably did when facing a tough decision, she drew a line down the page to form two columns, one of which she labeled pro, the other con. In her usual meticulous style— *why didn't I approach the partnership this way?*—she listed the arguments on both sides, then sat back, biting the eraser as she studied her work. Finally, she reached a decision.

She dialed a telephone number and listened as the phone rang. Just as she was about to hang up, a woman's voice answered with a hesitant hello.

"Hello, Ginny," she said to her birth mother. "Sarah Mathews calling."

"I saw that from the caller ID."

"How have you been?" Sarah asked.

"Fine. What do you want?"

That was direct. "Nothing, really. We haven't spoken since —it's been over a month, hasn't it? I just want to keep in touch."

"Okay," Ginny said.

Sarah waited for more, but when nothing was forthcoming, she said, "How is your work going?"

"Fine," she said. "It's a job. Listen, I have things to do, so if you have nothing more...."

"You were looking for a photo of Paulie," Sarah said.

"I told you we weren't much for pictures."

"But you promised to ask other people for snapshots."

"Did I? I haven't had time."

"He was my father. I'm naturally curious."

"I'll ask Eleanor," Ginny said. "She may have something."

"That would be nice." Then, getting to the point, Sarah said, "Have you given any more thought to coming here for a visit?"

"No," Ginny replied. "I can't get away just now."

"You must have some vacation coming?"

"What little time off I get, I save for the holidays."

"For the weekend, then?" Sarah said. "We should have invited you for Memorial Day."

"I couldn't have come. I'm caring for David."

"You could bring him. He must miss his mother. There's lots for a boy his age to do here. How about the July 4th holiday? Both of you can stay with us. We have a pool."

"I'll think about it," she said. "I have to go now."

"I understand, but try to come. We need you here. Nora misses you."

"Not really. She's doing well there. We talk every evening. She's fine."

The last time they talked, Ginny had said she seldom heard from Nora. Now they talked daily. Or was that just a story?

"You don't need to worry about her," Ginny said.

"I'm more worried about you," Sarah replied. "You must feel abandoned."

"You needn't worry about me, either." Something in Ginny's voice suggested she had seen through Sarah's attempt to get her to intervene with the woman she had raised to bring her back to Fessenden.

Sarah wished her well and ended the call. *Mission not accomplished.*

~

Sarah had prepared a Chinese chicken salad for dinner. As they sat on the back patio, she ate in silence, poking at her meal without eating it.

"Something wrong?" Victor asked.

She let out a long sigh and said, "After dinner. This may take some time." While Victor cleaned up, she gave Kellan his bath, watching as he floated a toy tugboat in the water, shouting "Toot-toot." She dried him off and dressed him, carried him into Victor for his goodnight kiss, and sat at the edge of his bed to read him *The Very Hungry Caterpillar*. He never tired of the story and enjoyed poking his finger through the holes the caterpillar created as he ate his way through the pages.

"Good night, Little Man," she said as she bent to give him a last kiss and cuddle.

"Not night yet, Mommy," he said, looking at the summer light oozing through the blinds.

"It's late," she said. "Time to sleep."

"Read again. Pweeze."

She tried another book, but all he wanted to hear was the story of the voracious lepidoptera. She began to read, but his eyes closed when she reached Saturday's meal of cakes, pie, and ice cream, a pickle, cheese and salami, a lollipop, and a slice of watermelon, and she left the room.

"Finally," she said as she returned to the kitchen, bending over to slide the glass serving platter into the vertical storage drawer.

"You were going to tell me what's troubling you."

"Yes," she said with a sigh, wondering where to begin. "I had a conversation with Ginny today. It did not go well."

"Why?" As she began to answer, he said, "I'm not asking why it didn't go well. I'm curious why you called her."

"I thought I could bring her into the conversation about Nora."

Victor stood facing her, his arms folded, a stern expression on his face. "To get her to return home, you mean?" It was not a question.

"Something like that," she admitted. Seeing his unchanged expression, she said, "You think that was a mistake."

Victor uncrossed his arms, placed his hands on his hips, and peered downward from one end of the kitchen to the other. "I thought," he said, "you were staying out of it. You said Lilly would have to work things out with Nora on her own. 'I'm devoting full time to my family.' That's what you said."

"I did, but I—"

"You promised."

"Don't you see what Nora is doing?" she said, her voice rising.

"Of course I do. She's trying to ingratiate herself, to work her way into this family, though for what reason I don't quite get."

"Money," she said. "She's after their money. And to get it, she's decided to get rid of me."

"But what *you* don't see," Victor said, placing both hands on her shoulders and looking into her eyes, "is that every effort you make to undermine her only strengthens her position. You've seen how Lilly reacts when you take Nora on. Your behavior risks driving a wedge between the two of you. You must let this play itself out."

"What if it doesn't?"

"Then it doesn't. There's nothing you can do to change it.

But your attitude will determine your future relationship with Lilly. You will either be part of a threesome or be on the outside looking in."

Sarah's nod was nothing more than an attempt to mollify him. *Whenever three women gather, one is left out,* she thought.

"Promise me you'll drop this fixation. Try to get along with both of them. Can you do that?"

"I'll try," she said. "I promise."

Ten

SARAH ENTERED Lilly's kitchen through the garage entrance, as she usually did. Standing at the counter sipping a latte, Nora looked up and said, "What are you doing here? We weren't expecting you."

A half-dozen responses came to mind, but, refusing to be intimidated, Sarah replied, "Replenishing the supply," as she dropped a loaf of rye bread on the counter. "Where's Mother?"

"Making herself pretty," Nora said.

"She already is." Sarah took the stairs to the upper level and entered Lilly's bedroom. The older woman sat before her vanity, accentuating her eyebrows with a light brown pencil.

"Hello," she said. "What brings you here?"

Was even Lilly making her feel like an intruder? "Kellan's in daycare this morning. I brought some bread over."

"Thank you, dear. You're always so thoughtful."

"I thought we could visit."

"We're going out in a few minutes, but have a seat."

Sarah scooted an armchair next to her. "You look lovely. Where are you two going?"

"There's a film about Ireland on the big screen at the Science Center," Lilly said.

"Afterwards, we're having lunch in Shadyside." Sarah looked up to see Nora leaning against the doorframe.

"That sounds lovely," Sarah said. "I wish I could go with you, but duty calls."

"What did you want to talk about?" Lilly said.

"Nothing, really. I just wanted to see how you're doing. How's Dad? I haven't talked to him in a few days." The two exchanged pleasantries, Nora hanging on to every word and Sarah wishing she could separate the two. She had come with no agenda other than having a moment alone with Lilly, but Nora seemed bent on turning their duet into a trio.

As her mother dressed in a light summer blouse and an ankle-length skirt, Sarah pondered how to get Lilly off on her own. Because Nora was still in her bare feet, she had an idea. "Your peonies are still in bloom," she said. "Aren't they usually gone by now?"

"Not always," Lilly said. "But with all the heat so early in the summer, I'm surprised they're still blossoming."

"Remember when we planted them?"

"You were still in high school. It seems like only yesterday."

"We got no blooms for a few years. I was so disappointed."

"You kept feeding and watering them," Lilly said. "I tried to make you leave them alone."

"Let's go look at them," Sarah said.

"I've just dressed."

Sarah reached for her hand. "It's still cool out. Come on, Mother."

She almost dragged her down the stairs and out to the deck, then down the stairway to the lawn. Lilly held her hand as they walked, and for a moment, Sarah felt all was right with the world. "It's been such a long time since we talked, just the two of us," she said. "We used to have these long conversations."

"And then Kellan came along," Lilly said.

"We still talked then. We used to sit in my living room while I was nursing him. And even this winter, we had some heart-to-hearts. I miss those moments."

"And you got busy with that TV show of yours."

Why is she avoiding the issue? Sarah wondered. "Has Nora told you when she's returning home? Her son must be out of school by now."

Lilly bent over the peonies, lifting a few of the stems whose buds touched the ground. "Get me the clippers," she said. "They're at the back of the top right-hand drawer in the kitchen."

Sarah knew where they were. "Can't we just—?"

"Go on, now. This was your idea."

Bowing her head in frustration, Sarah turned and headed toward the house. She hadn't taken ten steps when Nora passed her. "What beautiful flowers," she exclaimed. "We should bring some in."

"Sarah's getting the cutters," Lilly said. "Let's brighten the house up."

Nora broke into an off-key rendition of "Brighten the Corner Where You Are" as Sarah approached the house. She closed the door behind her, resisting the temptation to slam it. Passing through the den, she saw Nora's cellphone resting alongside Lilly's, a symbol of their togetherness. She entered the kitchen and, as she reached in the drawer for the clippers, spotted Lilly's purse on the counter. The top was open, a yawning chasm of makeup, combs and brushes, tissues, and her wallet with its profusion of credit cards. *Not a good idea, leaving that out in the open.*

She returned with the clippers and stretched them out, handle first, toward her mother. Nora intercepted her, snatching them from Sarah's hand and handing them on. As Lilly bent over among the flowers, Nora huddled over her, blocking Sarah from the woman she'd always considered her mother.

Her hands shaking in frustration, Sarah sat behind the wheel of her BMW, running the engine to keep the car cool. The church parking lot was empty, save for those of the daycare workers inside. It was twenty minutes until noon, and parents wouldn't arrive to pick up their youngsters for another fifteen minutes. She tented her arms over the steering wheel and buried her head in them. She hadn't imagined things. Nora had poked her nose into every conversation, skulking in the background and interjecting herself into every exchange. In the garden minutes before, she had interposed herself between Sarah and her mother, destroying a rare moment of intimacy between them.

And Lilly had allowed it to happen. Was she permitting Nora to intrude on their private discussions, or was she oblivious? Either way, Nora was trying to claim primacy in Lilly's affections, and it was working.

The emptiness she felt at that moment—there was no other word for it—was intensified by the fact she had no one to share it with. Lilly had always been her confidante, and now she had no way of reaching her without Nora's interference.

She had shared her growing uncertainty with Cheryl, but Sarah's attorney had put her off-limits until they resolved their dispute over the partnership. If it ever would be. The pandemic and financial collapse of the fitness clubs had separated Sarah from her former work colleagues, not that she had ever confided in them. She knew a few other parents at church, but was not close enough to dump her problems at their feet.

And then there was Victor, the husband who should be supporting her but failed to understand how she felt. Two nights before, his exasperation apparent, he had made her promise to get along with both Nora and Lilly. He didn't understand how impossible this had become.

Dear God, please help me. Weeping to herself, she pounded her fist on the steering wheel, producing a series of loud honks. And a tapping at the car window. She rolled it down and stared through tear-stained eyes at a sweating member of the grounds maintenance crew.

"*¿Está bien, señora?*"

"Yes," she said. "I'm fine. Thank you for asking."

"*¿Necesitas agua?*"

She looked up at his crinkled features, his face contorted with concern. *The only adult who cares about me.* "I have a bottle," she said, holding it up. "But thank you—*gracias por preguntar.*"

He returned her smile and gave her a hesitant wave. Other parents began arriving. Sarah pulled herself together, dabbing her eyes with a tissue. She got out of the car to collect Kellan, walking unsteadily as though she were drunk.

"When is your next lesson?" Sarah stared at the message on her YouTube channel and wondered how to answer it. It had been three weeks since she'd last posted an episode and two weeks since she'd turned over the final copy for the cookbook, the same day she'd received the letter from Cheryl's attorney. During the ensuing eleven days, they hadn't spoken. Under William Cartwright's instructions, she had not contacted Cheryl nor, presumably acting under similar instructions from her attorney, had Cheryl reached out to her.

Sarah's fingers paused over the keyboard while she thought. "Soon," she typed to her YouTube fan. "I've taken a little summer break, but I'll soon be back with more recipes. Many more."

But how was she to do that without Cheryl? She'd have to hire someone else to produce the segments, someone who preferred using their own video gear, someone who would be expensive. The production costs could make Sourdough Sal unsustainable.

This realization showed how much she needed Cheryl and how much she owed her. Despite her attorney's admonition, Sarah picked up her cellphone and clicked on the familiar number. Cheryl answered immediately, as though she'd been waiting.

"Hello, Sarah." Cheryl's voice was timorous.

"Hi." And with that, Sarah didn't know what else to say. An awkward silence followed, ended only when both began laughing. "This is absurd," Sarah said.

"Look, I'm sorry things have—"

"No, I'm the one who's sorry. I should never have...." She paused, fighting for the right words. "I should have listened to you. You told me what you needed, and I was so involved in my own problems, I didn't pay attention."

"Still," Cheryl said, "I shouldn't have lawyered up. All it's doing is costing us money."

"Which we don't have," Sarah said. The two talked for several more minutes until Sarah asked, "Have you heard anything? Where do things stand now?"

"No, Theresa Simon is going back and forth with your lawyer."

"Has she shared the financial statement with you?"

Cheryl gasped. "You sent it to her?"

"Days ago."

Cheryl insisted she hadn't seen a thing. "The way this is going, it could drag on for weeks."

"Months, even," Cheryl said.

A thought flashed across Sarah's mind, and she didn't take time to censor herself. "Let's fire the lawyers. I'll send you the financial statement. If you like it, send me the draft agreement, and I'll sign it. Sound good?"

"Sure...."

Sarah didn't need to see Cheryl's face to sense her hesitancy. "If you need me to advance you more, just say so. I'm not in this for the money."

"Okay, but...."

"What is it?" Sarah insisted.

"Since this all began, I've been sending out resumes," Cheryl said.

Sarah caught her sigh before it left her throat. "Any bites?"

"I have an interview next week."

"Good luck," she said. "Would that change our partnership?"

"Only if there's a non-compete clause. The agency didn't allow me to work for anyone else."

"Let's just hope...," Sarah began. "No, I wish you luck."

They agreed to tape another episode before Cheryl's interview and rang off. Sitting at her kitchen counter, Sarah folded her hands and closed her eyes as though in prayer. One step forward and two steps back.

～

As the organist played the offertory, Lillian Lindstrom reached in her purse. While her husband made a generous annual contribution to the church, no one seated near her knew that, and she couldn't bear passing the plate without putting something into it. As she peered into her wallet this morning, however, she frowned. Something was wrong. As Nora passed her the plate, Lilly withdrew a five-dollar bill—one quarter of what she usually contributed—laid it atop the few bills and sealed envelopes, and handed the offering to Sarah.

What she'd seen—or hadn't seen, to be more precise—so concerned her she paid little attention to the sermon and was grateful when the service ended. She spent no time visiting with others. Turning to Sarah, she said, "Do you mind if Nora rides with you?"

"Sure, Mom. Is everything okay?"

"I just need to spend a moment with Steven."

She grabbed her husband's hand and marched straight to his car. "Take the long way," she told him as he slid behind the wheel.

"What's wrong?" he said.

"Am I...?" The sentence caught in her throat.

Steven drove a half-mile, turned off on McLaughlin Run Road, and parked behind the country club, leaving the engine running. "What is it?" he asked.

"I want you to tell me the truth," she said. "Am I getting forgetful in my old age?"

"You are not old," he said. "And, no, you are not losing it. That's what you're asking, isn't it?" She nodded and drew a deep breath. "Sweetheart, what's going on?"

She gulped, staring out the window without looking at him. "I'm losing small amounts of money out of my purses. Nothing major. Ten dollars here. Twenty dollars there."

"Someone's taking it."

"I can't say that."

"Have you asked Nora about it?" When she didn't respond, he asked again. "Have you?"

"Not directly. I just... I noticed it Wednesday after we got back from lunch at Girasole. 'You know, if you ever need money,' I said, 'you can just ask me.'"

"What was her response?"

"She thanked me and told me how generous I've been."

"You didn't confront her?"

"Of course not. I don't know that she took it."

"Who else would have?"

Another pause, this one longer. "Sarah was over that day."

Steven snorted. "Why would Sarah do that?"

"Perhaps she wanted me to think Nora took it."

"Sarah would never do such a thing. Don't even think about it." His tone was dismissive, negating any response. "You're certain you didn't spend it elsewhere, leaving a tip after lunch?"

"No, I put it on the card. I've checked."

He put the car into drive and made his way toward their home. "I take it more is missing now."

"Forty dollars," she said, "nearly all I had."

He said nothing for a few blocks. "You need to keep it with you, your money. Keep it in your pocket or something."

"Say nothing to Sarah about this," she said.

He didn't answer her, but she hoped he'd heard her. She didn't want to accuse anyone, but it bothered her that Sarah had been sitting alongside her throughout the service. Could she have reached into her wallet while she wasn't looking?

Throughout Sarah's life, Lilly had been her confidante. She hid nothing from her except for sex. And that omission was only because the topic was one Lilly neither discussed nor wished to discuss. As films and television had become more open—"coarse," is how Lilly put it—she had turned to vintage movies and spent hours watching the Hallmark Channel.

With this exception, no topic was off the table, and the two women had formed a bond unusual among mothers and their grown daughters. Now Sarah had no way of reaching her without Nora's interference. Even when she called Lilly on her cell phone, Nora got the context from Lilly's end of the conversation and would chime in. "Put her on speakerphone," Nora had demanded days before. And Lilly had done so.

As Sarah sat at the counter of her kitchen set planning her next taping, the growing isolation from her mother preyed on her. How was she to break through the wall Nora had erected? On an impulse, she picked up her cell phone and texted Lilly. "I need to speak with you. Can we meet somewhere, just the two of us?"

Perhaps Lilly would assume she was having marital difficulties and give her the privacy she requested. Putting her phone down, she tried to resume plotting the steps she should need to take to record an episode featuring sourdough brioche, but her conflict with Nora kept dragging her away.

What does the woman really want? She had told Victor that Nora was just after money, but that wasn't the entire story. She wanted control. But why? Power for its own sake? As compensation for the life of privilege she felt had been denied her. She'd said enough to suggest that was the case.

What about Ginny? Why did she seem content to let Nora, whom she had raised, lust after a family that had done nothing for her? Not only did she appear to accept the situation, she also had taken on the role of caregiver to Nora's son. David was out of school for the summer, but Nora had made no move to reconnect with him. Why? And why did her family seem content with it?

Behind it all loomed the figure of Eleanor Frangos, whose effort to construct her family tree had started all this. Why was she so contentious, treating Sarah like an enemy?

I'm missing something. Something is going on that I don't see.

She realized she was holding her phone again, tapping its end against the work surface. As she halted the nervous motion, the phone chimed, signaling a message. "What is this about?" she read.

Should she make up some story or be direct? "I'd rather tell you in person."

"We can come over now if you'd like."

How thick you are! Can you not read? "Just you," she wrote. "I need to discuss this in private."

There was no immediate response, and Sarah returned to blocking out the episode. The sourdough starter would have to be thicker for this recipe since the dough contained much more liquid than the typical bread recipe. As a result, the levain would be heavy. She planned the steps she would have to take before the taping, now two days off, and then planned how she would stage this before the cameras. After a few minutes, she fell into the familiar rhythm—recipe, my preparation, the presentation. One-two-three.

Again, the phone chimed. "Why can't Nora come? We have nothing to hide from her."

Jesus! "Mother, this is about Nora. We need to talk privately. I have deep concerns."

There, she thought. *Now I've done it.* Sarah wished for a moment she'd been more circumspect, but after considering her options, she decided she had none. *I have to sit back and see what happens. It will tell me everything I need to know.*

She finished her plan and began typing the steps of the lesson into her computer. She would enlarge the font, printing each series of steps on legal-sized paper to guide her during the taping. Her phone rang. She answered after seeing who was calling. "Hello, Nora," she said.

"I have erased your angry message," she said. "Your

behavior has distressed mother. You have no right to upset her. You need to seek counseling to get over your anger."

She did not wait for an answer, but disconnected the call. Sarah's heart raced. Her face flushed as blood raced to her head. Not only had Nora closed off her one way of reaching Lilly, she was reading her messages. She had broken into her phone somehow and now controlled what she was allowed to see. Sarah had promised Victor to leave Lilly and Nora to their own devices. She now had no intention of doing so. Nora had to be stopped.

Eleven

SARAH FINISHED her lesson with a flourish. "Now there's a brioche," she proclaimed with a sweeping gesture encompassing the entire counter. "I'm Sourdough Sal. Here's to more baking in the wild."

She held the pose until Cheryl yelled, "Cut!" From behind the light box, she said, "That was great. One of your best."

"Thanks," Sarah said. "If this turns out to be my last episode, I wanted it to be memorable."

"I hope it won't come to that. If I get an offer, I'll try to make certain we can continue to do these."

The two women, friends again, embraced, and as Cheryl began packing up the video equipment, Sarah cleared the kitchen. The taping had gone so smoothly she'd surprised herself. For two days, she'd thought of little more than how to loosen Nora's hold on Lilly. She'd tried reasoning with her and confronting Nora. Neither had worked. Lilly was so isolated Sarah couldn't get a private word with her. Not that it would have done much good, for Lilly remained blissfully unaware of what Nora was doing to her.

She realized she'd made a tactical error. By distancing herself from the two women, she'd brought them closer together. She would have to reinsert herself into their lives. And so, with an hour to go before she picked up Kellan, she took the finished brioche loaf with her and parked in the circular driveway of Lilly's house.

She let herself in through the garage entrance, placed her gift on the kitchen counter, and was about to issue a cheery hello when she heard loud voices from the den. She crept toward the door and listened.

"I would like to help," Lilly said, "but Steven says we can't afford it."

"But how am I to get around?" Nora asked in her quiet, little girl voice. Sarah imagined her painting the air with her hands.

"I'll take you wherever you need to go."

"But I can't ask you to take me everywhere." Sarah heard a pleading note enter Nora's voice.

Lilly did not respond. Sarah could picture her staring around the room in confusion, something she did when she didn't know how to deal with an unpleasant topic.

"It's like being a prisoner here," Nora said.

"Oh, don't say that." Sarah could hear the hurt in Lilly's voice.

"I just mean...." Nora began. She didn't complete the thought.

"I understand, dear," Lilly said. "You can borrow my car whenever you please."

"Thank you, Mom. But I need to become more independent. I can't continue to rely on you for everything."

Gag me, Sarah thought. She retraced her steps across the kitchen without making a sound, then opened the door to the garage and slammed it shut. "Hello," she called.

Lilly entered, stepping into Sarah's outstretched arms while Nora trailed behind. Freeing her mother from her grasp, Sarah took a step back. "What's wrong?" she said.

"Oh, nothing," Lilly said.

"Have you been crying?"

"I got something in my eye. It's the season. Allergies, you know?"

Sarah looked past her at Nora, frowning, knotting her eyebrows together as though interrogating her. "We were just having a discussion," Nora said.

"About...?"

"Oh, nothing, really," Lilly said.

"It must have been something," Sarah insisted.

Nora shrugged. "I'm feeling a bit trapped, is all. I need a car so I can get out on my own."

"Why not?" Sarah said. "So, what's the problem?"

Lilly and Nora greeted her with silence as they looked at one another. Lilly broke the spell. "She needs help with it."

"That's no problem," Sarah said, assuming her most innocent demeanor. "Victor can help. He knows a few dealers. What are you looking for?"

"A BMW," Nora said.

"Whew!"

"It's not just the brand of car," Lilly said. "She needs help with the financing."

"Talk to the bank," Sarah said, frowning as though she didn't understand the problem. Then, as the two women continued to exchange glances, she added. "You mean you need money?"

"Yes," Lilly said. "But Steven refuses."

Sarah rubbed her cheek while considering her next move. "Why don't you just rent a car for the short time you'll be here?"

The glance Nora and Lilly exchanged told Sarah all she needed to know. "You're not returning home, are you?"

"No, like I said, I like it here."

"Where will you stay?"

"Here for the moment, but I want to bring David up by the end of the summer. The schools are better here."

"And he'll move in with Lilly and Steven?"

"For a few weeks, at least, until he gets to know his grand-parents."

Throughout this brief discussion, Lilly said nothing, turning her head back and forth between the two of them as though they were playing table tennis. "And how do you feel about this?" Sarah asked

"We have room," Lilly said. "This place is too big for just the two of us." Not only did this not answer the question, it was a sentiment her mother had never expressed before.

"It's just for a few weeks," Nora said. "Then I'll want a place of our own."

Nora could not afford an apartment in Upper St. Clair, and the schools elsewhere might be no better than those in Fessenden. Sarah couldn't figure out what she was thinking. "Are you looking for a job?" Sarah said, returning her atten-tion to Nora. "Because if you want your own car, you'll make monthly payments on the lease and insurance. You'll need money for an apartment, food, and clothing."

"I'll find something." Nora snapped out her response like the tail of a whip.

"You might want to do that before you think about a car."

"Now, Sarah," Lilly began.

"I'm just trying to help, Mother." Turning back to Nora, she said, "A BMW is beyond your budget. My first car was a Honda Civic. I paid for it myself, remember, Mother?"

"You had a lot of advantages," Nora shot back. Absent was the meek, tranquil voice.

"I watched a pair of neighborhood kids five days a week after school. I earned enough to put money down and made the monthly payments."

"Steven helped with the insurance," Lilly said.

"So I was on the family policy. Everything else I did on my own."

Her response elicited only silence. Nora stood with her arms folded, an angry expression on her face. Lilly frowned, looking from one girl to the other. Sarah thought she would begin weeping at any moment.

"Why not consider a lease? You make a substantial payment up front, but the monthly payments are lower than if you purchase outright."

"That makes sense," Lilly said in an apparent attempt to smooth the waters.

"That's decided then," Sarah said. "One of Victor's clients owns the Honda dealership. I'll ask him to put some figures together. Do you have a car in Fessenden to use as a down payment? No? We'll figure something out. But right now, I have to pick up Kellan."

Sarah left before either woman could say a thing. She stewed to herself as she raced up the road to the church. This couldn't continue. She needed help. Perhaps Steven would intervene. They had not discussed Nora for a month. He had then offered nothing more than sympathy, but that was when they both thought Nora was about to return to West Virginia. Now that she had decided to stay, it was time she met with him again.

~

Once she dropped Kellan off at daycare the following morning, Sarah appeared unannounced at Steven's office at Eagle Energy. She told the security guard she'd come to surprise her father, and once Janice, Steven's assistant, cleared her, she took the elevator up to his office.

"This is a delightful treat," Janice said. "He's been working on something all morning and needs the distraction." She tapped on his door and said, "Someone to see you."

As she stepped aside, Sarah entered. Steven looked up, startled, shoveling what looked like copies of newspaper clippings into a file folder. "What's that?" she said.

"Just records of an old case I worked on." He slid the folder into the file drawer behind his desk. "I'm reliving past triumphs," he said. "I'm getting too old for this."

Only then did he rise and give her his customary hug. "Don't be silly," she said. "You're indestructible."

"I wish my body agreed with you. What brings you out in all this heat?"

She smoothed her skirt and took a seat in one of his padded armchairs. "Are you aware Nora has decided to stay?"

He knitted his brows, a slight frown playing across his face. "For how long?"

"Permanently. She plans to bring her son with her later in the summer. They're moving in with you until they get their own place."

She did not imagine it. Steven's hands shook as he brought the tips of his fingers together. "What makes you think so?"

"Lilly told me yesterday." She waited as his eyes studied the surface of his desk. "She hasn't mentioned this?"

He hesitated before answering. "Perhaps I wasn't paying attention."

"Perhaps she hasn't mentioned it because she knew you'd object."

Normally, he would have torn into her for questioning Lilly's sainthood, but he said nothing, staring in her direction but not, she thought, looking at her.

"Dad, I haven't wanted to bother you with all this, but

that woman is destroying my relationship with mother." She led him through all she had experienced over the past few weeks, Nora intruding on every conversation, blocking Sarah in the garden days before, and intercepting and deleting the text message to Lilly. She struggled to keep her voice flat, emotionless, although inside, she was quaking with pent-up frustration and rage. "And Lilly is letting her do it," she concluded.

Steven bent over, resting his forehead on his right palm. She could see him breathing deeply as he thought. After an interminable silence, he said, "Your mother is angry."

"At me?"

"No, nothing like that. She doesn't like to talk about it, but—. Has she ever told you what she went through before you were...?"

"Born? No."

He rose and stared out the window toward the hills above Kennedy Township. "We tried hard to have a baby, but she couldn't bring it to term. She had two miscarriages and one stillbirth. A boy. Seven months into her pregnancy. It nearly killed her. Not physically, but emotionally. We would go for walks and see couples our age wheeling baby carriages, fathers playing catch with little boys, mothers pushing their daughters on swings. She would burst into tears right out in the open before God and everyone."

He jingled coins in his pocket, still looking out at the summer haze blanketing the landscape. "And then she got pregnant again. At 39 years of age. This would have delighted most couples, but we were terrified. We thought we'd lose another baby. I knew what it would do to her. It was months of living hell."

"She's never told me this," Sarah said, trembling. "I knew you tried to have children. She always called me her miracle baby, but miscarriages? A stillbirth? I didn't know."

He turned to face her, and she saw tears in his eyes. "I had no business taking her with me that Thanksgiving Day. She wasn't supposed to be traveling. Her doctor had told her to take it easy, do no housework, just sit and wait. Given our ages, we weren't only worried about another stillbirth, but about birth defects, developmental issues, you name it."

She held her breath. Until Kellan was twenty months old, he hadn't spoken a word. No Mama. No Dada. Just grunts and cries. In a panic, she had scoured websites, researching brain damage, autism, and other causes of late development, ignoring her pediatrician's reassurances he was a perfectly normal child. She could only imagine what imaginary terrors Lilly and Steven had conjured up.

"I was trying to repair a terrible relationship the company had with its miners, so I invited every family to a Thanksgiving Day dinner; we held three of them, as I recall. I asked her to come along, and despite her condition, she agreed. Maybe she was doing it to support me; perhaps she was just glad to get out of the house. I don't know. But it was a mistake. She went into labor in Fessenden, four weeks early."

He paused, drawing both index fingers below his eyes. "And I went on with the tour. The job was more important to me than her health or the birth of our child. She was angry at first, but took so much joy in you she soon got over it. Or suppressed it. I don't know which. The presence of a baby girl after all those years brought her back. You saved her," he said. "It's why the two of you are so much closer than most mothers and their girls. You were — are a part of her.

"And then," he said, "this."

Sarah's thoughts were spinning. "I'm not who she thought I was."

"Don't put it that way. She loves you. The two of you share a bond nothing can destroy. But to learn, after all she's gone through, that the child she gave birth to was shunted away to some working-class family in the coalfields...."

"And denied the love, education, and advantages only she could provide," Sarah said.

"Exactly. So she's angry. Angry with me, angry at the clinic, angry at the world. Her rage has blinded her to what Nora is doing—isolating, manipulating, and stealing from her...."

"Stealing? Nora is stealing from her?"

"Twenty dollars here, forty dollars there. Nothing major."

Sarah pursed her lips. "Do you know about the car?"

"The BMW?" He gave a dry laugh. "Yes, Lilly had to talk to me about that one. I put a stop to it."

"Not quite," she said. She recounted their conversation of the day before. "I promised to get her a quote on a leased Honda Civic. I sent it to her this morning."

She withdrew from her purse a printout she'd received from the Honda dealership hours before. "It's $3,399 at signing, plus $38 for vehicle registration," she said, "then $209 per month."

Steven shook his head. "That will not happen," he said.

"How will you stop it?"

"I don't know yet, but I'll think of something." He clenched his hands. "We are not buying that woman a new car."

She returned home minutes later, reflecting on all she had learned. Lilly, consumed with guilt over the life Nora had been forced to lead, was giving her anything she wanted while ignoring the woman she had raised and manipulating her husband for abandoning her on the day of that birth.

And where, she wondered, *does that leave me?*

~

After lunch, Sarah coaxed Kellan to lie down for a while. He had developed an aversion to afternoon naps but was willing to lie in his crib and play with stuffed animals. Despite his best intentions, he sometimes fell asleep, but not today. As he sat in his bed chattering—how she loved to hear his little voice and frequent giggles—she called Cheryl.

"How did your interview go?" she asked.

"Fine, but they didn't make an offer. They may have other candidates, but I'm keeping my fingers crossed."

Sarah processed her response. Of course, she wanted this job. Why else would she have applied?

"Did you ask whether we can continue doing YouTube videos?"

"I didn't ask. I don't want to jinx my chances by raising side issues."

Cheryl had already told her the opening was with WTAE, the local ABC affiliate. "What will you do for them?" Sarah asked.

"Graphics for the morning and noon newscasts. It's an early shift, and," she added with a chuckle, "Lord knows I'm not a morning person."

"It doesn't sound exciting."

Cheryl's sharp intake of breath told Sarah she'd said the wrong thing. "It's a job," she said.

"I didn't mean it like that. I just want you to feel fulfilled."

"Fulfilled? I'm more interested in keeping my belly filled." Her voice took on an edge as she added, "Or are you more concerned about yourself?"

Sarah felt like she'd been slapped. "No," she said, "I'm concerned for you. You're my friend, and I want what's best for you. If this is it, I hope you get it."

"I'm sorry," Cheryl said. "I didn't mean that."

"You did, but I deserve it." Sarah kept forgetting the two women were at different levels on Mazlow's hierarchy of needs.

~

Sarah spent her afternoon preparing ratatouille, and when Victor returned at 5:30, the smell of eggplant, tomatoes, and garlic filled the house. He embraced her from behind as she pounded pork chops flat, preparing to bread them. "You're doing all this in the summer heat?" he said.

"Careful, I still have the mallet in my hand."

"How did your day go?" he asked.

"I ambushed Steven," she replied, accurately describing what she had intended and what she'd done. "Lilly hasn't bothered to tell him Nora is moving in."

"How strange," he said as he uncorked a bottle of rosé and poured them each a glass.

"I thought so, too, but then he gave me insight into Lilly's state of mind."

She repeated the details of their struggles to have a child, the miscarriages and stillbirth, and her anger now that she'd learned a nurse had exchanged her miracle child for another woman's baby.

Victor removed his reading glass and looked into her eyes. "How does that make you feel?"

"Like shit," she said. Tears welled in her eyes, and she let them flow. "He insists her feelings have nothing to do with me, that they love me as much as ever, but it hurts. It hurts bad, Victor."

He took her in his arms. "I understand, Honey. I really do. Maybe...," He rocked her back and forth in his arms. "We should get away for a while. Take Kellan out west for a few weeks. Have you ever been to Vancouver? British Columbia is the most beautiful spot on the North American continent."

"I'm not leaving," she said between muffled sobs. She dried her eyes on a hand towel and contemplated the flattened cutlets. "I won't run away from this. I'm going to fight it."

"How do you propose to do that?" he asked.

Sarah poured safflower oil into a large frying pan and raised the heat while she thought. She didn't know what to do, just that she needed to do something. "She's stealing from her," she said.

"Who?"

"Steven told me Nora is taking money from Lilly. All this, when Lilly gives her any damn thing she wants. And now this car."

Victor shook his head but said nothing. They ate in silence, Kellan tearing into the thin bites of pork she'd cut for him. He turned up his nose at the ratatouille, so Sarah rose and blanched some broccoli for him. He wouldn't touch the stems, but loved to nibble at the flowers. She pondered the problem as she sliced the broccoli into small bites and slid them onto his plastic plate.

"I'm going to spy on her," she said. "I'm going to pop in whenever I can and pay close attention to what's happening."

"I wish you wouldn't."

"And why not?" It was less a question than a challenge.

"You'll take time away from your business—"

"That's on hold until Cheryl figures out what she's doing."

"—And," he said, repeating his mantra, "you risk alienating your mother."

"Maybe you're right," she said. But she'd made up her mind, and nothing Victor could say or do would change it.

Victor and his father had never been close. He had left the family when Victor was nine and, although he had provided well for his family, he had left his son with an aching chasm in his soul. They'd had a rapprochement for a time when his father thought Victor would follow in his footsteps and become a physician, but when the son went his own way, the rupture had become complete.

Now, months after they'd last spoken, Victor called the man. They spoke for a moment, exchanging awkward civilities, then Victor got to the purpose of the call. "I want to ask you something, and I need an honest answer. Why," he continued, without giving his father a chance to react, "did you divorce mom?"

His father waited several seconds before answering. "That's between us. It's really none of your business."

He suppressed the urge to shout at the man, to tell him it was his business. But he kept his anger inside him, as he always had. "I've heard Mom's version. I need to hear yours."

"Oh, so she's telling tales," he said. "We'd agreed not to involve you kids."

"We're no longer children. I just want—I need to hear your side of the story. It's important."

His father scoffed. "I suppose she claims I left her for Lois," he said. His father had married his nurse a year after the divorce, but that marriage, too, had dissolved. "It's not true. We got together after your mother and I split. She saw a lonely man and thought he'd be her meal ticket." It was all Victor could do to contain himself. *Always someone else's fault*, he thought. "Then what?"

"People drift apart," he said. "When you're having a successful career, the world looks different than when you were young and struggling. I had grown during my years in medical school. Your mother had not."

Now Victor could not restrain himself. "She was putting you through school," he said. "While she was raising your family and paying your bills, you were enjoying personal growth."

If he meant his words to shock his father, they did not. "You see what she's done to you," he said. "I supported my family. I put you all through school. You've never thanked me."

"Thank you," Victor said, "for your time."

Clasping his hands behind his neck, he leaned back in his chair and studied the ceiling tiles. *I never had a father*, he thought. *Never had a man to teach me to play catch, fly a kite, or how to ride a bike. Even when you were there, you weren't there. I'll never do that to my son. No matter what happens.*

~

Sarah poured herself a cup of coffee and sat at the breakfast table across from her father. "What brings you here so early?" he said.

"I've been delivering fresh bread in the morning and thought I might catch you," she said.

"Lilly told me you'd been stopping by more often. Good for you." He took a long sip from his coffee mug, emblazoned with a photo of Kellan and the words Best Grandpa Ever. "What's on your mind?"

Sarah looked behind her as though someone might eavesdrop, then, in a quiet voice, said, "They're still sleeping, aren't they?"

Steven chuckled. "You know your mother. She's never awake before nine, and Nora sleeps even later."

He was telling Sarah nothing she didn't already know. For a week, she'd arrived earlier each morning, testing how late Lilly's day began so she could explore the house on her own. This morning, she'd prevailed on Victor to watch Kellan for a few hours, claiming she was having breakfast with girlfriends from church. She'd been surprised to find Steven still at home but had settled across from him as though that's what she'd intended.

Now the surprise encounter gave her an idea. "I've been thinking about the missing money," she said. "I know Lilly has her own checking account. Have you checked to see how much she's transferring to Nora?"

"No," he said, drawing it out as though thinking about it. "Your mother has her own money from her parents' estate. When she asks, I help her move funds from her savings account into checking, but I don't question how she spends it." He rotated his coffee mug. "Do you think I should?"

"You know her account is linked to Nora's?" she asked.

"I know she's giving her money, but I thought she was just handing her cash."

Keeping her voice down, Sarah explained how Lilly had asked her to connect the two accounts so she could transfer money whenever Nora needed it.

"Then why would Nora go into her purse for money?" He also lowered his voice, taking on a conspiratorial tone.

She inverted her palms. "I'm not sure. Perhaps she's asked for more than Lilly is willing to give her. But," she said, stroking her forehead with her fingers, "that makes no sense. If she were stealing hundreds of dollars, that would be one thing, but twenty dollars here or there? It doesn't add up."

"I never look into her accounts unless she asks me to," Steven said as he drained his cup. "She doesn't handle money well, so perhaps I should. Though without evidence...,"

"How could you even broach the subject?" she said, completing his thought.

"Exactly. Let me give this some thought, but right now," he said, glancing at his Movado chronograph, "duty calls."

They gave each other a quick hug, and Steven scooped up his wallet and phone and entered the garage. She waited until she heard his SUV back out and the garage door close behind him, then washed out their breakfast plates and coffee cups while she thought about their conversation.

Slipping off her pair of Rothy's flats, Sarah padded around the ground floor barefoot, listening for any sound of life. Finally, she entered the den where two iPhones—Lilly's and Nora's—lay side-by-side at the charging block. She glanced around her while she debated. Then, holding her mother's phone close to her body as though to shield it, she opened the banking app, entering the code she had memorized the day she'd set up the transfer. Five hundred here, six hundred there. Lilly was transferring substantial sums to Nora at least once a week.

She closed the phone and considered whether to continue. Again, she glanced around, then grasped Nora's phone, entered the passcode, and opened the banking app. She whistled to herself. There was less than a thousand dollars in the account. Where was the money going? She paged through the charges to Talbots, Nordstrom, several other high-end stores, and almost daily debits to Starbucks. Despite these charges, a bit of addition told her the expenses didn't match the income Lilly was providing.

She focused on several other charges, recurring transfers to another account. Whose, she couldn't tell, but she suspected Nora was sending money to West Virginia. Just like refugees wiring money home to Central America, she thought. With that, her anger grew. She doubted Lilly had any idea she was supporting Nora's family.

The woman had grabbed onto Lilly like a leech. It was, just as she had suspected, all about money. Sarah knew she should close the app and return the phone to its resting place, but curiosity drove her on. She opened the messaging app and scrolled through the conversations. Several were with Eleanor and Ginny, Nora's comments in gray and their responses in green. Most were banal, but if she'd had time, she suspected she could peer into Nora's thinking.

She was more interested in the most recent thread, this with David, her ten-year-old son. "I love you and miss you. Mommy's sending more money tomorrow," read a gray text.

Back came the reply in blue. "Luv you too."

"What are you doing?"

Shielding Nora's phone with her body, Sarah clicked the right-hand button and placed the phone at the charging block. She removed her own from her hip pocket and turned to Nora, who stood ten feet behind her. "I forgot to charge my phone last night. I was disconnecting yours to get a boost."

"Dad's cable is right alongside it," Nora said. There was no mistaking her accusatory tone.

"So it is," she said.

"What are you doing here so early?"

"Steven and I had breakfast together. I brought a loaf of Swedish limpa. Can I fix something for you?"

Nora advanced, reached behind her, almost shoving Sarah out of the way, and detached her phone from the cable, balancing it in her hand as though to take its temperature. "I can fix my own," she said.

Sarah shrugged. "Suit yourself."

"You really shouldn't be here when Mother's not up."

"I was raised in this house. I lived here until I got married, so I don't need your permission to be here. Or anywhere else, for that matter."

"It's like you're snooping on us."

Sarah felt herself warming to the conflict. "Why?" she said. "Do you have something to hide?"

"I don't, but you do."

Sarah scoffed. "Tell my mother I came by to see her," she said.

Nora followed her through the den, into the kitchen, and

out the garage door, watching with arms folded as she got into her car and drove away. Only then did the blood rush to Sarah's head and her hands shake. How long had Nora been downstairs? Had she watched Sarah slink through her finances and phone messages? Worse yet, had she overheard the conversation with Steven?

She recalled Victor's warning: *No good can come of this.*

Twelve

THROUGHOUT THE INDEPENDENCE DAY WEEKEND, Sarah held her breath, expecting a call from Lilly demanding to know what she had been doing at the house a few days before. Why had she been going through their phones? Had she looked at her bank accounts? But she heard nothing. Nora seemed to have kept what she suspected to herself.

After church Sunday, she had the family over to her house for a cook-out. Victor grilled burgers and hot dogs while Sarah splashed with Kellan in the pool. She planted Nora at one end of the outdoor table while she sat at the other. Few words passed between them, and if Lilly sensed the tension, she didn't mention it.

Steven, who sat alongside Sarah, glanced toward Nora, then made eye contact with her, raising his eyebrows and communicating his contempt for the interloper. She shook her head, warning him off. If he kept this up, Nora would see it. Sarah could imagine her ruining the holiday by accusing them of conspiring against her.

Apart from this, the day passed without incident. Nora

even rose from the table to carry the dishes inside, the one time Sarah had seen her lend anyone a hand. However, as she thought about it, she decided this was Nora playing Janus, showing Lilly her dutiful-daughter face.

"That went well," Victor said when they'd left.

"You sound relieved."

"I am. I kept waiting for something to happen."

"Me too," she said, and with that, recognized the tension she'd been under all afternoon, waiting for an accusation, a cutting remark, a confrontation of some sort that never came. Perhaps she'd gotten away with it.

But Sarah had another problem. She had not told Victor about her surreptitious search of the cellphones. To do so, she would have to admit she'd lied to him about having breakfast with girlfriends on Thursday morning. She had always been open with him, and he, as far as she could tell, with her. She had hidden this from him—done what he'd warned her not to do with nearly catastrophic results—which added to her disquiet.

When Victor left to play a poor game of golf on July 4, leaving her alone with Kellan, she spent the day fretting. Something was bound to explode, but she did not know where and how it would present itself.

After she and Kellan splashed in the pool, she took off his floaties and sat him beside her to play with his toy dump truck. His small voice imitated the roar of an engine. She mulled over her situation as she lay back in her lounge chair. Nora had Lilly in her claws. Steven knew it but was unwilling to intervene, except where it came to money matters. Victor had counseled Sarah not to interfere, but if she didn't, who would? Her attempt to probe Nora's financial transactions had come close to disaster. How could she make Lilly see what was happening without losing her?

A sudden splash brought her upright. Kellan was flailing

at the water. She tumbled out of her lounge, scraping her knees on the surface, reached for him as he thrashed with both arms, then dove in as he sank.

"Oh, my God," she cried as she lifted him onto the lip of the pool. Kellan shook, coughing as he gasped for air, his eyes blinking in fear.

Her fear turned to anger. "Don't you ever do that again!" she shouted.

He burst into tears, his body heaving until his crying retreated into sobs.

She hopped out of the pool and took him in her arms. "I'm sorry, baby. It's my fault. I wasn't watching. My fault, not yours. Mommy is so sorry." She enveloped him in her arms, matching his cries with her own.

What is happening to me?

~

The following morning, Sarah had almost recovered from her fright. She didn't tell Victor what had happened, but he noticed the scabs forming on both knees. "What happened to you?"

"Oh, I tumbled out of the lounge at the pool," she said. "Nothing more than carelessness." Had Kellan been a bit older, he might have told his father what had happened, but he appeared to have forgotten about it.

Not Sarah. The guilt was a weight around her neck as she cleared the breakfast dishes the following morning. *I have to let this go,* she decided. *It almost cost Kellan his life.*

But it would not let her go. At mid-morning, Lilly appeared at her door, a frown plastered across her usually placid face.

"What a pleasant surprise," Sarah said. "Where's Nora?"

"I left her at the salon," she said.

"Just the two of us, then. How nice."

Sarah offered her coffee, but her mother declined. "One more cup and I'll go into arrhythmia," she said.

"Are you having heart problems?" Sarah said, suddenly alert.

"No, I was just—" She scooped Kellan off the floor and sat him on her lap. He wriggled away. "He's growing up too fast."

"You don't know the half of it," Sarah said. "So what occasions this visit? Not that I object."

Lilly hesitated. "Maybe I will have a little something. Some juice?"

Sarah poured a glass of apple cider and sat across from her in the breakfast nook. Lilly took a sip, then pushed it aside, staring across the kitchen as though seeking a cue card. "I'm missing money," she said.

"Really? How much?" Ten dollars here, twenty dollars there, Steven had said.

"Several hundred dollars."

"Mom! How? When?"

"I noticed it this morning when I stopped by the bank to withdraw money for our trip to the salon. They don't take credit cards, you know."

"Money is missing from your checking account?"

Lilly nodded. "I took Nora to the salon but backed out, saying I wasn't feeling well. I told her to call me when she's finished. Then I returned to the bank."

"And?" Sarah prompted.

"Four hundred fifty dollars was transferred from my account on Thursday and into Nora's."

Sarah noted the passive voice. Money was transferred, not Nora transferred it. Stole it. "What will you do?"

"I don't know. I need to talk to someone about it, and I can't...."

"Tell Steven? Why not?"

"He thinks I don't manage my money well. He might accuse Nora of taking it."

"Why shouldn't he?" Sarah demanded. "It went from your account to her account. It didn't just take wing and fly."

Lilly took another sip of the apple cider. Buying time, Sarah thought. "Who else would have taken it?" she asked.

With tears in her eyes, Lilly said, "I suppose you're right."

"I am right. Mom, I suspect you're giving her quite a bit of money. What's she doing with it?" Sarah had to tread carefully here. She knew Lilly was giving Nora regular cash infusions; she also knew Nora was sending much of it to her family in West Virginia. But she couldn't say so, for to do so would reveal she'd pried into both their phones.

"I've been transferring money to her. You set that up. She has no other income now, but she's looking for work." Suddenly, she brightened. "I probably sent her that money Thursday morning and forgot about it. Maybe I'm losing it."

"You are not 'losing it.' Stop blaming yourself. You would have remembered transferring that amount of money."

"No, I think that's the explanation. Nora would never do anything like that."

"But, Mom—"

"Thank you for listening," she said, sliding out of the bench to rise to her feet. "You're always such a help, dear. And please don't tell your father about this. I don't want him trying to manage my money."

When she hesitated, Lilly said, "Promise me. Don't mention this to Steven."

"All right, Mom, but I want you to keep a close eye on your account."

"I will. You keep your promise, and I'll keep mine."

With that, she floated out the door, leaving Sarah swearing to herself in frustration. She had to alert Steven, but to do so, she would cut her fraying ties to the woman she loved.

~

"I got the job," Cheryl said as they met at the Starbucks in the Galleria mall.

"Congratulations," Sarah said, though she wasn't sure how she felt about it. "When do you start?"

"Monday."

"That soon?" She lifted the paper cup of cappuccino to her lips to hide her expression.

"Yeah, they've been paying tons of overtime and want to get me started."

Sarah raised her eyes in silent inquiry.

"I have to get through a three-month probationary period," Cheryl said. "If they like my work, they'll give me a contract."

"They'll like your work."

"But here's the thing," Cheryl continued. "As I feared, the contract contains a non-compete clause."

Sarah's heart went colder than her coffee. "So you can't work for me."

"With you," Cheryl corrected her. "Not after the trial period."

Sarah nodded, taking that in. "So, what do you want to do?"

"Oh, I'm taking the job."

"Of course. What I mean is, can we work together for the next three months?"

Cheryl frowned as though she'd not thought about that. "I don't know. I thought you might want to dissolve the partnership."

Sarah had not considered this possibility. "You've invested a lot of time and effort in Sourdough Sal. Even though we're not yet showing a profit, our fans continue to buy stuff, ad revenue is coming in. We'll be in the black soon. And you're a part of it."

"But now you'll want to partner with someone else—someone like me."

"There's no one like you," Sarah replied. "If I continue the channel, I'll hire a production crew, not bring on another partner."

But in that case, Sarah realized, Cheryl would end up profiting from work in which she wasn't involved. No, she needed to pull back, think about this, and talk with an attorney. Not William Cartwright this time. Someone else.

Cheryl leaned closer and lowered her voice. "You said if you continue. You're thinking of giving it up?"

Sarah had not thought that far off. She'd given the matter almost no thought, consumed by the family drama embroiling her.

"I don't know," she said. "I'll have to consider my options. You, meanwhile, start your job and don't worry about any of this. I'll figure something out and get back to you."

"Okay," Cheryl said, a smile lighting up her dark features.

"Again, congratulations," Sarah said, and this time she meant it. "You'll be a rock star."

The two friends embraced, and Sarah left, driving down Washington Road until she reached Bird Park in Mount Lebanon. Leaving her phone in the car, she hiked down the trail into the park while she thought about her future.

Sarah returned to her BMW with her mind at ease. For an hour, she had wandered through the nature reserve until an idea took shape. What she'd come up with so appealed to her she picked up her phone to research its potential. Instead, a flurry of text messages greeted her. "When are you picking up

Kellan?" one read. Two more became insistent. "I have to leave. Please pick up your son."

She raced up Washington Road, cursing as the two-lane highway turned into one lane through what a perpetual construction project. She reached the church, only to find the doors to the daycare center locked. She peered through the window, but there was no one there.

She raced through the hallway to the church office. "They've left," the secretary said. "They close at noon." She cast a meaningful glance over her shoulder at the clock, which read 12:45.

Sarah's skin felt clammy, yet perspiration rolled down her sides. Where could he be? Standing just inside the door to the parking lot, she paged through messages and calls on her phone. Nothing.

Victor would know what to do. She dialed his number. One ring. Two. Then his voice. "I have him," he said.

"Thank God. I'm so worried. I was meeting with Cheryl and lost track of the time. Victor?" She held her phone away from her ear. He had ended the call.

Sarah drove the short distance home. Victor stood in the kitchen, slicing an apple onto Kellan's plate. Her son's eyes lit up when he saw her, but her husband did not acknowledge her presence. "I'm sorry," she said. "I got wrapped up in work issues."

He said nothing.

Raising her voice, she said, "I was worried sick. You might have called me."

He turned and fixed her with a venomous gaze. "Don't turn the tables," he said. "I was in the middle of a walkthrough with clients when the school called. It was twenty minutes past noon. They'd been trying to reach you, but you didn't answer. I picked up Kellan and then called Lilly. No one knew where you were."

"I'm sorry I —"

"And you say *you* were worried."

Slumping, she dropped her arms. "Victor, I'm truly sorry. Something came over me. Cheryl's taking this job and won't be able to work with me. On top of this thing with Lilly, I just —"

"I don't care."

"What did you say?" Sarah scowled. Tears flooded her eyes.

He grabbed her arm, pulling her out of the kitchen and into the dining room, pulling the pocket doors closed.

"You heard me," he said in a low voice containing a hint of menace. "I don't care about Cheryl." He swept his arm before him and said, "I don't care about Lilly, Nora, or any of this. All I care about is this family. Our son, whom you left at daycare, was frightened and crying because he saw how upset the staff was."

"It won't happen again."

"Kellan tells me he 'drowned, but Mommy saved me.' What's that all about?"

"Oh, God!" she cried, holding a hand to her mouth. "It was Monday. We were at the pool. He was right by my side, but got away from me and jumped in. I heard him right away and jumped in after him."

"Remember how angry you were with me at Ohiopyle?" he said. "Where were you all this time?"

"I was lying on the lounge chair, thinking about things."

"What sort of things?"

She took a deep breath. "Something happened at Lilly's last week, and I was worried she would find out."

"*What* happened?" His voice was icy, demanding.

Slowly, it all came out. How she'd gone to Lilly's the week before after telling him she was having breakfast with friends. How she'd gone through both cell phones, looking for financial transactions, and how Nora had caught her with her hand in the cookie jar.

Victor listened to her recital in silence. "Is that it?" he said when she'd finished. She assured him there was nothing more, that she'd told him everything.

"Then here's what's going to happen." He neither frowned nor smiled. His jaw was set, and he stared at her with such intensity she felt forced to look away. "You will drop this obsession with Nora. Whatever is going on between them, stay out of it. When you're around Lilly and Nora, behave yourself. No more sniping. No more sneaking around. No more calling her family in West Virginia. Is that clear?"

She nodded, but said nothing.

"You are to keep an eye on Kellan. If you have to leave him, call me. I will watch him, pick him up, and do whatever needs doing. But you have to let me know. Got it?"

He was treating her like a child—no, like his property. She had never known the man she loved to speak to her this way. Anger rose, and she prepared to fire back.

"Because if you don't," he continued, "I will leave and take Kellan with me."

She opened her mouth, then closed it. He meant what he said and had the means to follow through with it.

Sarah stumbled through the weekend as though she were carrying a fifty-pound sack on her back. After church on Sunday, they gathered at Lilly's house. "What's wrong?" her mother asked. "Is something bothering you?"

In an earlier time, she would have unburdened herself. She and Lilly had once been so close. But to tell her Victor was angry with her—had threatened her with divorce—she would have to reveal the reason. And like peeling an onion, as she had revealed layer after layer of the story, she would have revealed that she'd opened her mother's phone and Nora's, snooping into their financial records. That she had done so to protect Lilly wouldn't have mattered. Her mother would have been furious over the invasion of her privacy. "Why didn't you just ask me?" she would have asked.

If she were honest, she would have responded, "Because I don't trust you to tell me the truth."

She could tell her mother none of this. "Cheryl is taking a job that will keep her from doing my production work. I'm just preoccupied."

To show Victor she was obeying his instructions, she fawned over Nora, asking her how she was doing, how her search for a car was going, and what she'd heard from home. She was so obsequious that, as they made drinks in the kitchen, Victor said, "You can stop now."

"I'm only trying to make nice."

"You're doing too good a job of it. You come off as though you're planning something or have something to hide."

"Yes, master," she said as she carried Steven's gin and tonic out to him.

She spent the rest of the afternoon feeling disconnected, an outsider looking in on someone else's family. Only Kellan seemed a part of her, and before dinner, she took him for a stroll around the lawn, pointing out new blooms in coral bells and salvia. She chattered to him as though he were an adult. "They don't get it, Kellan. No one sees what's happening. I feel alienated from everyone. You're all I have."

He favored her with a grin, pleased to be brought into her confidence. He hugged her leg and said, "I wuv you, Mommy."

She got down on one knee and embraced him. "My little man," she said. "I love you, too. It's just the two of us, you know. Just we two."

The day passed without rancor. "You did well," Victor said as they reached their house.

"I'm glad you approve, master."

"Sarah…," he began.

"Please drop it. I'm doing what you demanded of me, and I'll continue to do so. Whatever happens, happens."

~

Sarah was on the phone when Steven knocked at the back door. She smiled and motioned him in as she continued the conversation. "End the YouTube channel?" she said. "I won't do that, not after all the work I've put into it. I've built a following."

She listened as the person at the other end argued with her, placing a mug before her father and reaching for the coffee carafe. He waved it away, and as she looked at him, she saw he was upset. "Look," she said, "I promise to think about it, but I have to go now. I'll call you back tomorrow at the latest."

She listened to the response and disconnected. "What's up?" she said to Steven.

"Sit down," he said. "This will take a moment."

She sat on the other counter stool and twirled it to face him. "Has something happened to Lilly?"

He gave a quick nod and inhaled. His blue eyes were cloudy this morning, and for the first time, Sarah realized his blond hair was turning gray. "Nora's gotten into her bank account," he said.

"I know." She took a quick gulp from her juice glass while considering how much to say. "She asked me not to tell you, but since you've already discovered it…,"

"When was this?" he said.

"A week ago. It was something over four hundred dollars, I think. Lilly didn't accuse Nora; she just said it was missing.

But by the time she left, she decided she'd forgotten giving it to her. That's not right, is it?"

Steven sighed and planted both fists on the table. "I wish she'd told me. I could have put a stop to it. Now, it's worse."

Leaning on the counter, she cupped her hands over her eyes as though shielding them from the sun. "How much worse?"

"How much is due on the Honda lease?"

"Just over four thousand."

"Nora transferred $4,037 from Lilly's account to her own Sunday afternoon."

"Hold on a sec," Sarah said. She flipped through a notepad on the counter's edge. "That's the amount due at signing, plus the registration fee. This happened while we were all together?"

Steven cleared his throat and nodded. "That was more than she had in her checking account, but since she had over-draft protection, the bank transferred the balance from her savings."

"Incredible. What are you going to do?"

"That's the problem," he said.

"Lilly doesn't want to call the police." Sarah didn't pose it as a question. She knew the answer.

"She does not. I'm working with the bank to reverse the transaction, but it's Lilly's account, not mine, and she seems paralyzed."

"What does Nora say about this?"

"She claims to know nothing about it." He snorted in derision. "She says she never uses the banking application."

"And you don't believe her," Sarah said, unwilling to tell him she knew this was untrue.

"I do not. She's on that phone all the time, scrolling, texting...."

Although he'd refused the offer, Sarah reached for the mug

again and poured him a cup of coffee, sliding the sugar bowl toward him. He heaped two teaspoons and stirred without saying another word.

"How is Lilly taking this?"

"She's in denial. Says Nora would never do such a thing. She was reluctant to raise it with her, so I had to confront her." Steven sighed and stared into his coffee mug for a moment. "In her heart, Lilly knows Nora took the money. She just doesn't want to face it. All her illusions shattered."

"So, what will you do?" Sarah demanded.

His shrug was almost imperceptible. "Lilly doesn't want to turn her in, so there's not much I can do."

"Dad!" He recoiled at the vehemence in her voice. "She stole money. She'll do it again if you let her get away with it now."

"The bank has unlinked the accounts, so she won't get another chance."

"She'll think of something else." Her voice raised, Sarah counted off the incidents on her fingers. "She took small amounts from Lilly's purse. Then, she increased the amount to forty dollars and more. When that wasn't enough, she transferred over four hundred to her own account. Now she's taken over four thousand. Face it, Nora is a kleptomaniac, and she's found a willing victim."

"I know," he said.

Sarah leaned over the counter, brought her face inches from her father, and peered into his eyes. "Why are you being so passive? Nora has done this before and will do it—or something like it—again. She has to be stopped, and if Lilly won't do it, you have to."

"It's really up to Lilly. It's her money."

"Then convince her." Hating herself for betraying the sisterhood, she played her ace. "You're the man of the house. Tell her she has to report it. It works, believe me."

She'd said everything but tell him to man up. He pulled back from her intense gaze, gulped down his coffee, and said, "You're right, of course. I'll take care of it."

He thanked her and left, leaving Sarah to wonder whether he would follow through and why, from the moment Nora had descended on their family, he'd been so reticent about speaking up. In a way, she blamed Steven for this, for he had let it happen.

Thirteen

VICTOR ARRIVED home to find Sarah had prepared a light supper of lobster tails on a bed of lettuce, a loaf of freshly baked French bread, and a bottle of champagne. "What's the occasion?" he asked.

She put Kellan in his booster chair at the table and served him a dinner of chicken fingers and broccoli while keeping her husband in suspense. When she finally sat down, she said, "Steven came to see me this morning. Before you say anything, I had nothing to do with this. He showed up at the door while I was speaking with an agent. He appeared to be so concerned, I rang off."

Sarah took him through the conversation. He asked no questions while she spoke and made no comments. Only when she'd finished did he say, "I don't get it. Why would Nora do something so brazen?"

"Good question," Sarah said. "I suspect she thought there'd be no consequences. She wanted a new car. Steven didn't want to pay for it, but Lilly wanted her to have it. So she figured if she just took the money out of Lilly's account, she wouldn't tell Steven."

"But that's crazy," he said.

"To you and me, maybe, but not to Nora. She's audacious."

Despite himself, Victor chuckled. "That describes her. So what does Steven intend to do about it?"

"He says he's going to make Lilly report the theft," Sarah said. "We'll see if he follows through."

"You don't seem so sure."

Balancing a bite of lobster on her fork, she said, "I'm not. From the first, he's been unwilling to act on his instincts about Nora. It's like she has some sort of hold on him. I don't get it."

"Paternal instinct, perhaps?"

She took her bite while she thought about it. "No, unlike Lilly, he seems to feel no attachment to her. There's something else."

Sarah chewed on the thought for a moment, then tossed her head, shifting her brown strands out of her eyes. "Anyway, now that they have found her out, I suspect they'll pack her bags for her and send her home."

"Making your day," Steven said.

"And I didn't have to do a thing. I did as you told me, stayed out of it. It was all Nora's doing."

"To Nora," Steven said, raising his glass.

"Nora," she repeated, clicking her glass to his.

Seeing them, Kellan extended his sippy cup. "Noah," he said. They both laughed, clicking their glasses against Elmo's image.

Nora Bouras sat on her side of the table, fidgeting with a handkerchief. Fred Newman, a criminal defense lawyer hired by Eleanor Frangos, sat alongside her, facing Ross Pennington, a detective with the Allegheny County Police Department who specialized in cases of grand theft, and his partner, Detective Patrice Morton.

"I swear I didn't do it," Nora said. Her body shook, and tears streamed down her face. "I took nothing from Lilly except what she offered me."

"She says you lifted money from her handbag on at least three occasions," Pennington said.

"I did not."

Laying two bank statements before her, Sergeant Pennington said, "Last week, you transferred four hundred fifty dollars from Mrs. Lindstrom's account to your own."

"That wasn't me."

The attorney examined the two statements. "You have no evidence my client made this transfer. Anyone could have done it."

"And on Sunday, you took another $4,037 from Mrs. Lindstrom's account and transferred to your own," Pennington said, "an amount equal to what you knew would be required to lease a new Honda Civic."

Nora screamed at the detective. "I didn't want that car. I admit I asked Lilly to buy me a vehicle, but it was a BMW just like Sarah's. Why would I want a piddling little car like this?" She waved backhanded in a dismissive gesture.

"You transferred these funds through a banking app on Mrs. Lindstrom's phone."

"I don't know how to use her phone," Nora said. "I wouldn't know how to get into it."

"Mrs. Lindstrom says you were present when Mrs. Mathews set up the app," Detective Morton said. "She claims she did so at your request."

"I never — Well, maybe I did ask her. Mother was giving me cash, but I needed a better way to manage it. By opening a bank account for me, she could transfer money whenever I needed it. That was her idea, not mine."

Pennington persisted. "Even before you made these transfers, Mrs. Lindstrom had given you over three thousand dollars. So where did the money go?"

"I bought things I needed. Clothes, shoes, a new purse, things Lilly wanted me to have. She took me shopping all the time."

"But she charged many of those items to her own accounts," Pennington said, turning pages in a case file. "What did you do with the money she gave you prior to last week?"

"That's none of your business."

"You sent it to your mother in West Virginia," Morton said. The detective didn't raise her voice, parrying each thrust with the facts. "Twenty-five hundred dollars over two months. You had Mrs. Lindstrom supporting your family."

"First off, Lilian Lindstrom is my mother. On the day I was born, nurses at the clinic handed her the wrong baby."

She was about to continue when the attorney interrupted her. "I advise you not to say anything more."

"But it's the truth," Nora said. "All these years, Lilly didn't know of my existence. She thought Sarah Mathews was her daughter, a woman who doesn't look like her, doesn't act like her, and doesn't think like her. So when my aunt untangled this mess, Lilly was beside herself with joy. She's showered me with gifts to compensate for what I was denied all these years."

"But it wasn't enough, was it?" Pennington said. "You wanted a car. Steven Lindstrom refused to buy it for you, so you took what you wanted."

"I did not, I tell you. I've never opened Lilly's phone. Sarah installed the banking app. I don't know how to use it."

"You transferred money to your family in West Virginia," Detective Morton said.

"By calling the bank and having them do it," Nora said. "I'm telling you, I don't use that app."

Attorney Newman half rose from his chair. "This interview is over," he said. "If you're going to charge my client with a crime, do so. If not, we're leaving. You have no evidence Nora Bouras took anything except what Mrs. Lindstrom gave her."

Pennington closed the file. "Interview terminated at Attorney Newman's request, July 15, 10:17 a.m." He shut off the recorder and told Nora, "We'll be in touch when we've spoken to the district attorney. Meanwhile, you are not to leave the state."

"I wouldn't think of it," she said.

Sarah sat across her dining room table from Lilly. Western Pennsylvania was under a storm watch, and dark clouds gathered on the southern horizon as the pair spoke. "I thought I had two daughters, the one I raised and the one I gave birth to. But all she did was take advantage of me."

Sarah reached out and covered Lilly's hand with her own. "I know you're hurting, Mom, but I'm here, and so are Victor and Kellan. We all love you."

Her words did not mollify Lilly. "I would have given her anything she wanted. She had only to ask."

"I know you would," Sarah said, and if Lilly heard the note of scorn in her voice, she did not react. "What will you do now?"

"I don't know." Lilly exhaled and looked past Sarah. "They've told her not to leave town, and she has nowhere else to go. So for the moment, she's staying with us."

"She should move into a hotel," Sarah said.

"She has no money."

Sarah gave a loud sniff. "Why is that your problem?"

"I don't know," she said, "but I can't just turn her out on

the street. She is my daughter, after all. Like it or not, she's a part of me."

"I understand," Sarah said, though she did not. The knowledge Nora had stolen from her should have been enough to sever the tie, but somehow Lilly insisted on hanging on, if only to a thread. "Still, it must be uncomfortable for you."

"I can't stand being in that house," Lilly said. "I can't even look at her. Fortunately, she spends most of her time in her room, but she has to come down for something to eat. I'm through waiting on her. I'd made her fix her own meals, but she leaves her dishes in the sink, expecting me to clean up her mess. I don't dare look in her room. I can't imagine what it looks like."

As if to punctuate her sentence, lightning flashed, the chandelier over the table dimmed, and thunder shook the house. Kellan ran into the room, reached out his arms, and climbed onto Lilly's lap. *My family*, Sarah thought. *I'm getting my family back.*

"What happens now?" Sarah asked.

"I don't know. The police are still looking into this. When they have enough evidence, the district attorney will file formal charges. It could take weeks." Lilly shook her head and bit the corner of her lip. "We know what she did. Noting can change that. I've told Steven maybe we should just drop the charges and send her on her way—get rid of her and this entire mess."

"That has a certain appeal," Sarah replied. She had no wish to be vindictive toward the woman. She just wanted her gone. "What does Dad think?"

"Oh, he's all for it, but I think this detective, Pennington, is his name. He's asked us to hold off until he completes his investigation. Why I don't know. If we're not pursuing the matter, isn't he wasting his time? And our tax dollars?" she added.

"Meanwhile," Sarah said, "you're in the middle."

"Indeed I am."

Sarah suggested she stay for dinner so she wouldn't have to face Nora. Lilly agreed, and Sarah put in a call to Steven to make it a foursome. "For that matter, why don't you move in here until she's gone?" Sarah said.

"And leave her alone in my house, doing God knows what?" Lilly said. "I can't let that happen. So we just have to wait it out."

Sarah heard nothing more from Lilly for the next three days. Steven, too, went silent. She considered calling them, but Victor had again asked her to stay out of it. "It's taken on a life of its own," he told her. "There's nothing you can or should do."

Despite the silence that grew louder as each day passed, she took his advice. She had plenty to think about. For months, an agent had been pestering her, insisting she could give her a better deal than she was getting through her YouTube channel. Sarah had investigated the woman and learned she had no track record. She was only a fan of the series who thought she could use Sarah to build her own business.

But she had decided the idea had merit during her walk in Bird Park three weeks before. She had emailed three agents representing other TV chefs to see what might lie there. One had expressed interest, but her advice was a bitter pill. "No production company wants you competing with yourself, so you must drop the YouTube channel."

As they met for a late lunch, she explained to Cheryl. "This means not only no new episodes, but withdrawing those we've already produced. So we'd have no more income, not from advertising, product sales, or the cookbook."

Cheryl winced. She'd poured her heart into the project, almost tearing the copy for the cookbook from Sarah's hands at one point. "What do you want to do?" she asked.

Sarah played with her Caesar salad while deciding how to present this. "With you no longer able to produce for me, I'm in a box. I could hire a production team, but that would cost more than the channel brings in. I could afford to operate at a loss for a while, but not for long."

Cheryl's cynical smile as she raised the glass of iced tea to her mouth told Sarah she'd seen the truth of the matter. Their partnership depended on Cheryl's work, which, if she were a private contractor, Sarah couldn't afford. Without her, there was no business.

"I propose," Sarah continued, "that we end the partnership, and I turn all the proceeds over to you."

Cheryl's eyes widened. "I thought we haven't turned a profit."

"We haven't," Sarah said, "but that's because I advanced money when we began so we could design the kitchen and purchase video gear. We're close to breaking even, but I can't continue without you."

"You're willing to take a loss to buy me out?"

"That's it," Sarah said. She slid a paper across the table, a spreadsheet showing what Cheryl would walk away with if she agreed.

"And what do you get out of this?"

After she declared the business loss on their tax return, the damage wouldn't be as significant as it looked, but that was none of Cheryl's business. "I walk away with a reputation as a baker and presenter I didn't have a year ago. I may be able to turn it into something. Then again, I may not. But without your involvement, I'm at a dead end."

Sarah had hardly touched her meal, but now took a few bites as she watched Cheryl process the offer, her eyes darting from Sarah to the spreadsheet and back. After a long silence, she said, "You're being too generous, but I need the money. I agree."

They finished their meal and parted, still friends. It was not the result Sarah had hoped for when she'd launched Sourdough Sal, but she'd proven something to herself, if to no one else.

Sarah awoke the following morning with a sense of loss. She faced a day in which she would tear down everything she'd built over the past several months, removing all lessons from the YouTube channel, closing her online store, notifying her corporate sponsors she wouldn't be promoting their products any longer, and removing the cookbook from online stores. It felt like burying a loved one.

Before she began, however, a telephone call changed the trajectory of her day. "My name is Detective Ross Pennington," the caller said. "I'm investigating the theft of money from your mother, Lillian Lindstrom. I'd like to ask you a few questions."

He asked her to come to the county police headquarters in Greentree. She was, as she told him, only too willing. *At last,* she thought. After asking Victor to drop Kellan off at daycare, she dressed and made the half-hour trip north.

She checked in at the reception area and was issued a badge to wear. The detective came out to meet her and led her to an elevator. He was a lanky man with swept back black hair and a nose that looked more like a crow's beak. "I'm glad you called me," she said. "Mother has been so upset by this."

He gave no sign that he'd heard her. "This way, Ma'am,"

he said as they exited the elevator. He led her into a small room with white walls. A rectangular table bisected the space, with two chairs on either side and a mirror on one wall. Pennington directed her to a seat facing the mirror while he sat across from her.

A woman entered the room, and he introduced her as Detective Patrice Morton. She was stocky with hair that was dirty blond on the strands and dark brown at the roots. Sarah had always pictured female detectives as young and beautiful, barely concealing their sexiness under official facades. She told herself she'd watched too many TV cop shows. Sarah extended her hand, but the female detective merely nodded as she took a seat alongside Pennington.

He began recording, stated the date and time, gave his name and that of his partner, and asked Sarah for her name. The scene seemed formal, but Sarah figured they had to follow protocol.

"Lillian Lindstrom is your mother, is that correct?" Pennington said.

"It is."

"And Steven Lindstrom is your father?"

"Yes, sir."

He led her through several other preliminary questions, which she answered. "On or about July 13, you had a conversation with Mr. Lindstrom. What did he tell you?"

She recounted what Steven had said about the money missing from Lilly's bank account.

"At that time, did you tell him you knew of another occasion on which money had disappeared?"

"Yes. Lilly has spoken to me the week before. As I recall, four hundred fifty dollars was missing on that occasion."

"Did you express an opinion as to who was responsible?"

"Of course. I told them Nora had done it, and both agreed."

Pennington asked a few questions, establishing who Nora was and her relationship to Sarah. "Why did you say Nora had taken the money?"

"We all knew she had done it."

"How did you know that?" Detective Morton asked.

"Because she'd taken cash from Mother's purse at least three times before, and Lilly had an app that allowed her to transfer money into Nora's account."

"But that was on Mrs. Lindstrom's phone. How could Nora have accessed it?" she asked.

"Because she watched me set it up."

"You set it up?" Detective Morris asked.

"Lilly asked me to do so, and Nora watched the process."

"But that doesn't mean she could access Mrs. Lindstrom's phone, does it? You don't know she had the passcode, do you?"

Sarah thought for a moment, then remembered. "I do. I sent Lilly a text message about a month ago. Nora intercepted it. She called to tell me she'd erased it."

"Can anyone corroborate that call?" Detective Morton asked.

"No. Nora called from her cell phone to mine. Since it dealt with Lilly, I doubt she was within earshot. And it was a quick call. She told me she'd seen my message, erased it, and accused me of upsetting her mother." Sarah snickered to drive home her contempt.

The pair glanced at each other, then resumed their questioning. "You and Nora don't get along, do you?" the woman detective said.

"No, but what does that have to do with anything?"

"Why do you dislike her?" she asked.

Sarah stopped in her tracks. "What's going on here? I thought I was here to help in your investigation into Nora's theft of money. What difference does it make why we don't care for each other?"

Pennington replied. "We're just trying to understand the relationship. What was the source of your disagreement?"

Sarah walked them through her history with Nora. How Eleanor Frangos's persistence had turned up a relationship neither she nor Lilly had known existed, how Nora had presented herself as Lilly's daughter, and how they had confirmed she and Nora had been switched at birth. "She moved in with them, insinuated herself into Lilly's life, gained her confidence, and worked to shut me out."

"Now," Pennington said, "on June 30, you came to your parents' house early in the morning. Your father was there. The two of you spoke, and then he left. Sometime later, Nora found you going through her cell phone and your mother's."

Sarah closed her eyes as a chill spread through her body. "I was trying to find out how much money Lilly had given Nora and where it was going. I shouldn't have, but I was protecting my mother. Somebody had to. Dad wasn't doing anything."

"And on that same day, $450 disappeared from Mrs. Lindstrom's account and went into Nora's."

"So I learned later, but if you're thinking I had something to do with it, you're way off."

"And on Sunday, July 10, you and your family had dinner at the Lindstrom's. After that, you disappeared for some time. No one knew where you were."

"I took my son for a walk," Sarah shouted.

"On that day, someone transferred over four thousand dollars from Mrs. Lindstrom's account into Nora's—an amount that matches what you had said was needed to set up an auto lease for Nora."

"I had nothing to do with that," she said, now aware of where this conversation was going.

"According to a journal Mrs. Lindstrom keeps,"

Pennington continued, "you were in her home or sitting alongside her in church on every occasion when money disappeared from her purse."

Sarah stared at one of them, then the other. "She's set me up," she said, her face draped in fury. "That bitch arranged this charade to get me out of the way. When my husband learned about the missing money, he asked me why Nora would have done something so brazen. Since Lilly was giving her everything she wanted, it made no sense for Nora to steal from her. Well, this is why she did it. She said she didn't know how to set up the banking app on her phone and that I had to do it for her. She insisted I establish her passwords and enter them. Then she began stealing, ratcheting up the amounts she took, and waiting for Lilly to react."

She pounded the table. "It was all done so she could take my place. She's done nothing for the past three months but complain about how she got the short end of the stick. My money, my education, my car, my career. She resented all I have, everything I've accomplished, and, most of all, my relationship with my mother. She wants it all, and she's taken you in."

Neither officer said a word, and Sarah realized she was digging herself in deeper. "I need an attorney, don't I?"

Both detectives stared at her for a moment without responding until Detective Pennington broke the spell. "The Lindstroms are deeply disappointed," he said.

"Distraught is a better word," Morton said. "It hurts them to think you would do something like this."

Another pause as Sarah soaked this in, the shame washing over her.

"But they are not pressing charges," Pennington said. "Mrs. Lindstrom has recovered all her money, and since you weren't the one who brought charges, we can't make a case against you for filing a false report. You're free to go, but they have asked us to make it clear they want no further contact with you."

"They'd like to continue visiting your son," Morton said, "and they'll arrange that through your husband. I don't recommend fighting them on this because you could end up in court, and no one knows what a judge might decide."

"So behave yourself," Pennington said, "stay away from Nora and the Lindstroms, and you'll be all right. Is that clear?"

Sarah nodded through her tears, but Pennington made her say it aloud. He ended the interview and stopped the recording.

Fourteen

WHEN HE HEARD Sarah's frantic summons, Victor closed his computer and headed home. He entered the door to find her sitting at the bar stool, slumped over the kitchen counter, supporting her head with both hands. "What's wrong?" he said. "You said it's nothing to do with Kellan."

"Oh, Victor," she cried. "They think I did it."

He stared at her in confusion for a moment, then said, "Did what? Taking Lilly's money? Who's saying this?"

"The police, but Steven and Lilly believe them."

"No," he said. "Take it from the top."

Between sobs and wringing of hands, she told him what had transpired, the questions the two detectives had posed that didn't go in the direction she expected, and her realization that they suspected her. "Victor, I didn't do this," she concluded.

"I'm sure you didn't."

"You believe me?"

Jerking his head back, he said, "Of course I do. You may have wanted to be rid of Nora, but you're incapable of doing anything so devious."

She buried her head in his chest, sobbing, and muttering her repeated thanks. "I wasn't sure how you'd take this."

He pulled away and stared into her eyes, his face inches from hers. "Sarah, I love you, and I trust you. Yes, I was upset when you failed to pick up Kellan and angry when he told me he'd fallen into the pool. But understand, I was also worried something had happened to you. When we couldn't reach you. I thought—" He broke off. "All sorts of things went through my head, sweetheart. I feared for your life. And when I understood all this was because you were obsessed with Nora, I told you to stop."

Looking downward, she turned her head from one side to the other. "If only I'd listened to you. If only I'd stayed out of this."

He nodded agreement but said, "This wasn't entirely your doing. Lilly told you she was missing money. Steven came to you when the four thousand dollars disappeared."

"Thanks," she said, wiping tears away with the sleeve of her blouse. "But how do I convince Lilly and Steven I had nothing to do with this? They believe the police, Victor. They've threatened to take us to court if I approach them or deny them visitation with Kellan."

Victor tapped the countertop with his index finger. "I'll talk to Steven," he said. "He didn't trust Nora from the start, so he's more likely to listen to reason."

But first, he wanted to give the man time to cool down. Victor did nothing for the rest of the day, staying home to care for Kellan to take the pressure off his wife. It proved to be the wrong strategy, for, with time on her hands, she moped about the house, breaking into tears at irregular intervals. He was at a loss about how to help her. Nothing he said mollified her, and as the day wore on, he wished he'd returned to work.

When he awoke the next morning, she was not lying alongside him in bed. He found her in the guest bedroom, wide awake and staring at the ceiling. "I couldn't sleep," she said, "and didn't want to wake you."

They splashed with Kellan in the pool. Then, a bit before noon, he asked if she'd be all right if he went off on his own for an hour. "Where are you going?" she asked.

He pulled a polo shirt over his head to hide his face while lying. "I left something at work when you called. I need to complete it."

Fifteen minutes later, he pulled into the country club and found Steven sitting with three friends in the Terrace Bar. Steven raised his eyebrows in silent greeting as he entered, but did not invite Victor to join them. He sat at the bar, ordered a burger, and waited.

Steven made no effort to end his visit, and Victor was about to give up when the first of the quartet rose to leave. Soon, the two others departed. Steven motioned him to the table, waving at the server for another gin and tonic. "What's on your mind?" he said.

"You know why I'm here. I'm here to talk about Sarah." When Steven did not react, he added, "Your daughter."

The older man shifted in his chair. "I'm deeply disappointed in her. That's all I can say."

"You've known her all her life. You raised her. She is incapable of doing something like this. She would never hurt Lilly."

The older man took a sip of his drink. "You should talk to Detective Sergeant Pennington. I can give you his contact information."

"I don't need to talk to him. I know Sarah. I love her, and I trust her."

"That's commendable. A man should stick by his wife. In sickness and in health, as the wedding vow goes."

Victor moved his face closer. "This is not blind loyalty.

Think this through. Sarah loves both of you. Her relationship with Lilly is precious to her."

"That's the point," Steven said. "She was afraid of losing her place in the family. She came to me more than once, imploring me to do something about Nora."

He emitted a long sigh and finished his drink in a gulp, patting his mouth dry on a napkin. "I blame myself for what's happened. Understand, I don't like the woman. Yes, she is biologically my daughter, but I feel no more a part of her than that waitress over there."

He signaled to her, pointing at his empty glass, worrying Victor he'd soon be trying to reason with a drunk. "If I'd been more firm with Lilly, none of this would have happened. I should have put up with this for no more than a couple of weeks, told her it's nice to get to know you, and sent her away. But I didn't. I allowed Sarah to pursue this—" He searched for the right word, then spat it out, "—Toxic relationship. I'll never forgive myself."

"And you won't reconsider?" Victor said.

Steven extended both hands, palms up. "It's out of my hands."

Victor rose from the table. "Okay, here's the deal. You and Lilly will see your grandson when you're ready to accept his mother. Not before. If you think you can take me to court over that, have at it."

With that, he walked away, unwilling to listen to whatever the man had to say.

Sarah settled into a daily routine. She took Kellan out of daycare and spent every day with him. She transferred her membership to a Presbyterian church in Bethel Park, where she met other young mothers. They set up a series of play dates, and Sarah's became the most popular destination because of their pool. When the families met at her house, she monitored the children, even hiring a high school swim team member as lifeguard.

In between showering attention on her son, she closed down Sourdough Sal and pestered her agent for any news about a deal. Sarah worried about driving the woman away, but whenever she texted her, the agent answered back within an hour. However, by the end of August, the agent had turned up nothing. Rather than growing discouraged, Sarah came to accept the verdict of the marketplace and turned to other interests.

As a child, she had always loved photography and now took lessons at the Apple store on creative ways of using her iPhone camera. She bought a small tripod and began taking time-lapse videos of cloud patterns. She took videos of Kellan and learned to edit them to document his life. Some days, she would sit next to him on the sofa to watch the movies, reveling in his excitement at seeing himself.

Small amounts of money continued to trickle in from past YouTube and store earnings; she sent them on to Cheryl, who thus remained a part of her life. The two met for coffee on those Saturday mornings when Victor could watch over Kellan for a few hours.

They vacationed in British Columbia. Sarah loved the bustle of Vancouver and the sweet smell of the breeze from the ocean air flowing in from the Strait of Georgia. She had never considered living anywhere but Pittsburgh, but this place drew her in. Then, as Victor drove west toward the Canadian Rockies, they spent a night in Penticton in the Okanagan Valley. Sarah didn't want to leave.

What she did not do was contact Lilly. Steven had made clear they had made up their minds about her, and nothing she could say or do would change them. By moving to another church, she had cut off all contact with them. She didn't know what Nora was doing, whether she had reunited with her son or where she was living. The Lindstroms seemed to accept Victor's decision, denying them access to their grandson. Kellan initially asked about them, but as weeks passed, he came to accept their absence. *Children are so adaptable,* she thought, *going with the flow. Unlike me.* Sarah knew this was cruel—to him and them—but so was their rejection of her.

The separation weighed on her. She did her best to put on a brave front, never complaining to Victor, but the estrangement from her family was like a knife in her heart. She no longer belonged to them, nor they to her.

To make matters worse, she heard nothing from her agent. She had given up the YouTube channel, hoping to turn her skills into something more significant. Now she had nothing. But, as the summer came to a close, she resolved herself to her new life.

With nothing but Kellan to occupy her, Sarah had time to brood about the events of the past five months. As her earlier suspicion that she was missing something weighed on her, it came to dominate her thoughts. Things she'd observed awakened her: Cheryl's message popping up on her phone in gray following her agent's text in green, how Steven had acted during her surprise visit to his office, and a gnawing conviction that something beyond money had motivated Nora to take actions that posed such a risk to her. She could have lost the battle.

On the first Saturday of fall, she acted. What she was about to do was illegal, as Cheryl had warned her while leading her through the process. But as Sarah entered Fessenden and parked before a narrow, two-story frame house, she assured herself what she was doing was right. She pulled to the curb, noticing a dark blue Honda Civic with a for sale sign in the window, rang the doorbell, and when she heard no sound, knocked at the door. A young boy answered. He looked about ten, was slender to the point of asceticism, and had a tangled mess of blond hair in need of clippers and a comb. He didn't speak.

"Is this where Ginny Bouras lives? Is she home?"

He took several seconds before answering, looking her up and down, his eyes blinking as though blinded by the sun. "She ain't here."

"When will she return?" Sarah asked.

"Don't know."

"I'm a relative," Sarah said. "I've come to visit."

She stepped inside before he could stop her, but he moved out of the way, raising no objection to the intrusion. "You must be David," she said.

He didn't answer her.

Peeling wallpaper didn't cover the living room walls, and the furniture was a mix of every style that had ever found its way into a thrift store. A recliner sat facing a flat panel TV set whose back was thicker than modern models, a wine-colored sofa with dark stains rested beneath the front window with a card table serving as a coffee table, and an armchair whose leather was peeling away sat just inside the door from the entrance.

Sarah took the chair while the boy draped himself across the sofa, paging through an iPhone. "Is that yours?" she asked. He didn't respond, poking at the screen as it emitted a series of beeps and sounds like someone shouting. He rocked back and forth to some unheard music. Earbuds, she assumed.

"Is that your grandmother's car in the driveway?"

Again, no answer. He's rude and undisciplined, she

thought. If he were my kid, I'd straighten his ass out in a New York minute.

Photos lined the stairway leading to the second floor. Taking the steps two at a time, Sarah began studying them. It didn't seem to bother the boy. Pointing to a portrait of a young-looking man with a head of curly black hair, she said, "Who's this?"

He glanced up without rising from the couch but didn't answer her.

"Is that your grandfather?" she asked. "Paulie?"

"Paulie," he said as he continued playing with the phone. "Paulie."

Sarah had now detected three lies—two from Nora and one from Ginny. She had another stop to make in this town and hoped Ginny wouldn't be long, but while she waited, she took advantage of the woman's absence. She backed against the railing, peering as far up the stairway as she could. Three photos of Nora were clustered together, one in a basketball uniform, another diving into a pool, and a third in which she wore a costume of some sort. As she took another step to get a better view of this photo, she heard a car pull into the driveway. Smoothing her slacks, she came down the steps. David didn't move.

"Hello, dear," Ginny called as she stepped through the door. Then, recognizing Sarah, her look of anticipation became a frown. "Oh, it's you."

"Yes. I had a meeting in Beckley and thought I'd stop by to say hello. I've been visiting with David. He's quite a boy."

She didn't respond to the description. David looked at the two of them, turned, and took the stairs to the second floor. Sarah was glad to see him leave, uncertain whether he knew hers was more than idle curiosity.

"Now that I'm here," Ginny said, "what can I do for you?"

Well, mother.... "Nothing, really. We had little chance to get acquainted, and since we're family...." Ginny stood in the doorway as though willing her to leave. "Have you eaten anything?" Sarah asked. "I could take both of you out for lunch."

"All we have here is a hamburger stand and pizza parlor." She stopped as though that settled things, but since Sarah didn't take the hint, she said, "I have some leftovers from last night. I'll rustle up something. I suspect you want to get back."

"I'm in no rush," Sarah replied, struggling to keep the annoyance out of her voice, "but I don't want to intrude." Which was precisely what she was doing. "What do you hear from Nora?"

Ginny didn't answer, but took off her cotton jacket, hung it on a hook behind the front door, and walked into the kitchen. Reticence appeared to be a family trait.

"You wait here," she called. "I'll just be a minute."

Sarah couldn't follow her without being detected, but despite the sound of pounding from upstairs, she heard Ginny speaking to someone in a low voice. Sarah knew who the person was.

She heard a microwave running, and soon, Ginny called her into the kitchen, placing two plates of steaming meatloaf and mashed potatoes onto a Formica table. Above them, the sound of someone hammering on the wall continued. Ginny walked to the bottom of the stairs and called, "David, stop that! David!"

Hearing no response, she stepped to the top of the stairs and shouted, "David, stop pounding the wall! Put on your headphones and listen to some music."

If he answered, Sarah didn't hear him, but the pounding ceased.

Returning to the kitchen, she motioned for Sarah to sit at the table. "Delicious," Sarah said after taking her first bite. She hadn't taken another when Eleanor Frangos burst through the front door without knocking. She was out of breath, having come running, perhaps literally, when Ginny called.

"What brings you here?" she asked in a demanding voice.

"I had a baking event yesterday evening with some of my followers in Beckley and thought I'd stop by."

"Where was it?" Eleanor demanded.

"A private home," Sarah improvised. She picked the most generic name she could think of. "Mary Alice Smith hosted it. Do you know her?"

"Huh-uh." Turning to her sister, she said, "You got any more of that?"

"No, I finished our leftovers. I can—"

"Oh, never mind," she said, taking a seat at the table. She crossed her arms. "So, what do you want?"

"I'm hoping you can tell me about my family." She fixed Eleanor with what she hoped was a guileless look.

They traced the family history, much of which Sarah had already heard, for a quarter-hour. When Sarah questioned them about Nora's childhood, Ginny left the table, returning with a high school yearbook. She proudly showed Nora's junior class picture, and Sarah was again struck by the young girl's resemblance to pictures she'd seen of Lilly as a teenager.

Ginny turned to photos of Nora's athletic achievements. "She made the state championship," she said. "UWV offered her a scholarship, but...."

She did not finish the thought, but Sarah felt she'd detected another lie. Ginny turned to a photo taken at a prom but quickly turned the page. "Who's that?" Sarah asked, turning back to point at the young man who stood with his arm around Nora.

"His name was Ralph," Ginny said. She and Eleanor exchanged glances as Ginny turned the page again, flipping past the following section without letting Sarah see it, then closing the yearbook.

"And what of my father, Paulie?"

"His father's name was Pavlos, Greek for Paul," Ginny said. "When he was young, his mother called him Paulie to distinguish him from his dad, and the name stuck. He was a good man."

"A miner, you said."

"Yes. He died young. There was an accident at the mine—"

"How long are you staying?" Eleanor interrupted to ask.

Sarah glanced at her watch. "Actually, I'd better get underway." She placed her phone on her chair, carried her dishes to the sink, and began washing.

"We'll get that," Ginny said.

Sarah picked up her purse, embraced Ginny, and shook hands with Eleanor. They stood on the front porch as she climbed into the BMW and continued up the street toward the highway that would carry her home.

Instead of turning right at the intersection, however, she crossed it and made her way back toward the center of the small town, thinking not about what they had said but what they had not. Neither woman had mentioned the theft of the money, the initial accusations against Nora, and the eventual determination that Sarah had engineered the theft to discredit her. Nora would have regaled them with the details, yet they'd not even hinted at it. And she was sure there were more lies than she'd already uncovered.

Sarah had come to Fessenden for answers to the questions that haunted her. She had now answered many of them, but she was convinced the rest—perhaps the most important— remained buried, hidden deep beneath the ground.

She turned into the parking lot beside the municipal building, pulled behind it where passers-by wouldn't spot the expensive foreign car, and entered the side door to the library. Sarah had tried to access past issues of the Beckley papers online, but they hadn't been digitized. She also wanted to study the small weekly in Fessenden, which had long since closed its doors. She knew what dates she needed to see and was soon sitting at a carrel going through microfiche of local newspapers from 2008 to 2009.

It didn't take long to find what she was seeking. She'd brought a roll of quarters with her she used to print copies of stories from eight back issues. For good measure, she asked for a copy of the 2012 high school annual. There were no photos of Nora. As Sarah suspected, Nora had gotten pregnant before or during her senior year and had not graduated.

With minutes to go before closing time, she called for the 2011 yearbook. There was Nora's class photo, the shot of her standing next to her beau—Ralph Gentry, according to the caption—who she took to be David's father. As the librarian flipped the light switch on and off, she turned to the last section, the one at which Ginny had abruptly closed the yearbook. She didn't need captions to find a photo of Nora as Emily Webb in the school's production of Our Town and another as Laura in The Glass Menagerie.

Sarah thanked the librarian and left, but before getting on the highway, she returned to Ginny Bouras's house. With rain drenching her, she ran to the door and pounded on it. Ginny opened up, her mouth agape. "I thought you'd left."

"I got as far as Sutton before realizing I left my phone here," she said.

"I haven't seen it."

"Do you mind if I look?" she said, breezing past the woman. "I had it with me in the kitchen. I sat right here and put it down while clearing the table. Oh, thank God, here it is." She picked it off the chair where she had left it, kissed Ginny on the cheek, and ran back to her car.

Sarah drove two blocks, turned a corner, and stopped, putting on her warning lights. She switched the car's audio to Apple CarPlay, opened the app Cheryl had loaded on her phone, and raced the audio ahead until she picked up the conversation.

Eleanor's voice boomed through the speaker. "Why the hell did you let her in?"

"I didn't," Ginny said. "She was here when I got home. David let her talk her way in."

Sarah drove another two miles while she listened, then pulled into the parking lot of a convenience store. She tapped the rewind icon and replayed one section.

"Oh, my God," she said. She sat behind the wheel shivering, weeping to herself. She recalled Nora's angry words as she had left Kellan's birthday party. "You don't know what it's like."

~

"Why the hell did you let her in?"

"I didn't. She was here when I got home. David let her talk her way in."

Steven and Lilly sat at Sarah's dining room table, Victor at the head, having ordered the couple to come over. Sarah had not returned home until ten the previous night. Victor was still awake, alerted by her frantic call from the road.

"I need you to hear this," she told him. He'd listened to the entire recording without comment, then sat in silence as she revealed what she'd learned at the public library.

"We have to tell them," he said when it ended.

"Yes, but how?" Sarah had wrestled with that question all night. As soon as she dozed off, more memories awakened her —Nora's sending money home, her attachment to Kellan, her amazement that he spoke so early when Sarah had worried about the pace of his development, and the change in Nora's manner when she wasn't in Lilly's presence. Hovering over it all, however, was Lilly's insistence that people make their own way in the world.

Over breakfast, she and Victor discussed how to break the news to Lilly and Steven, and after church, Victor had put it into motion by telling his father-in-law, "As soon as you've had lunch, I want you to make your excuses to Nora and come over."

Steven had resisted. "Lilly doesn't want to speak to Sarah," he said.

"She needs to hear this. You both do. While you're here, you can visit with Kellan."

Victor had no qualms about using his son as bait, if that's what it took, so when Steven still balked, he said, "If you're unwilling to do so, you'll never see him again."

The threat had worked. They had come reluctantly, not speaking to Sarah as they entered, playing with Kellan for fifteen minutes before Victor had ordered them to the table, where a Bluetooth speaker rested alongside Sarah's iPhone.

"I recorded a conversation between Eleanor and Ginny using an app that makes it appear the phone is off," Sarah began. "Taping someone without their consent is illegal under West Virginia law, so I'm putting myself in your hands. If you don't believe what you hear, you can turn me over to the cops. Again," she added for emphasis.

She pressed the play button, and the four listened to the two women arguing over how Sarah had gained access to the house. "Did she suspect anything?" they heard Ginny say.

"I don't think so," Eleanor replied, "but I wish you hadn't pulled out that yearbook. If she saw the photo of Nora in Our Town...."

"She didn't. I skipped over it."

"She's an intelligent woman," Eleanor insisted. "If she

discovers what an accomplished actress Nora is, she'll suspect something."

As their words filled the room, Sarah passed out copies of Nora's yearbook photos.

"What if she returns?" Ginny's voice asked. "Why is she showing such sudden interest in our family?"

"Just keep her away from here. If she asks to get together again, meet her in Beckley. Above all, keep her away from David."

The two fell silent for a moment as Ginny washed the lunch dishes. Sarah advanced the recording, glancing up to assess the couple's reactions. Lilly looked back and forth as though puzzled while Steven sat hunched forward, his hands in his lap and his brows knitted in concern. *He's getting it*, she thought.

"It won't be much longer," they heard Eleanor say. "The old man is still resisting, but Nora has Lilly wrapped around her finger. She'll bring him along like she did with the car."

"A BMW," Ginny exclaimed. "Who would have thought they would give her such an expensive vehicle?"

Eleanor brayed a laugh so harsh both Lilly and Steven's bodies quivered. "Steven pulls back the four thousand dollars, and Lilly makes him buy a forty-thousand dollar car. What a sap!"

They could hear both women chuckling. Lilly sat open-mouthed, but Steven sat with a vacant expression, as though he were viewing the scene from afar. His mood had changed, and Sarah knew why.

After the sounds of more clattering as they put the dishes away, Ginny resumed the conversation. "It isn't fair what you've done to her."

"Don't waste your sympathy on that woman," Eleanor replied. "I didn't like her from the moment she responded to my first message."

"But she is my flesh and blood. Why destroy her? Why be so cruel?"

"We had to get her out of the way—out of the will," Eleanor said, correcting herself. "And Nora did just what I told her, playing it perfectly. For the next ten years or so, she'll live in luxury. Once they're gone...." They heard her snap her fingers.

"And we deserve it," Ginny said. "Nora and David especially."

Sarah reached for her phone and stopped the recording. "There's more," she said. "Eleanor lays out exactly how she planned this as soon as she learned who raised me. I kept thinking of Nora in dramatic terms: Janus-faced, being caught in front of the curtain. How right I was. Eleanor wrote a script for the biggest act of Nora's life."

Raising her stubby Greek fingers as she counted off elements of the plot, Sarah said, "Nora worms her way into the family. She isolates Lilly, playing the role of the wronged, abandoned daughter while lying about her background. Nora didn't attend college because she was too poor. The Mountaineers had offered her an athletic scholarship. When she became pregnant, she lost it. She dropped out of high school and still doesn't have a diploma.

"Far from playing Little Miss Sunshine in my presence," Sarah said, her tone becoming venomous, "she became the Wicked Witch, stirring up discord to drive us apart. When that didn't work, she and Eleanor cooked up this financial hoax. Nora played the role of an electronic neophyte. She owns a late-model iPhone David now uses. She acted helpless, so I would have to set up the banking applications. You'll recall, Mother, she insisted I choose her passwords and open your phone to install the app.

"And then," she concluded, "she began taking money from you whenever I was around. Ten dollars, twenty, forty—

she kept ratcheting it until you noticed—then four hundred, and finally four thousand. All the while insisting the iPhone you bought her was too complex for her to use. She framed me to get at you."

"Why?" Lilly's voice cracked as she asked, "What did Ginny mean when she said we deserve it? I know Nora resents my taking home the wrong baby." She apologized to Sarah. "I didn't mean it that way."

"It's okay," Sarah said, "but you're wondering why Ginny would feel she's also been wronged."

As Lilly nodded, Sarah turned toward Steven. "Do you want to tell her?"

He returned her stare, then lowered his head. "Tell me what?" Lilly said.

"This began just as Eleanor claimed," Sarah continued. "She was constructing her family tree, took the DNA test, and discovered someone she'd never heard of: me. She reached out, trying to make sense of it all. When I resisted, she looked into my background and discovered a man named Steven Lindstrom had raised me. She knew that name, didn't she?"

Steven glanced at her, but looked away. His shoulders fell. "When Eagle Energy first brought me to West Virginia, there was an explosion at one of our mines," he said. "Several men died, including Paul Bouras. I suppose they blame me for that, and, when they discovered the clinic had switched babies, they saw an opportunity to get even."

He gave Sarah a look, imploring her to remain silent, but she had been through too much to let it go. "These clippings from newspapers in Charleston, Beckley, and Fessenden tell the rest of the story," she said as she handed a file folder to Lilly. "When Eagle bought these mines, they were in terrible shape and leaking money. They brought in Steven to bust the union. With their contract up and no progress made, the miners struck, but they couldn't hold out forever. When they admitted defeat and returned to work, Steven had stripped all their benefits. They had no health insurance, and their retirement program was gone. They had only what they could bring in by working long hours in hazardous conditions."

"Eagle's acquisition team failed their due diligence," Steven said. "We paid far more than the mines were worth and had to invest massive amounts in safety improvements. The money had to come from somewhere."

Sarah forged on as though he hadn't spoken. "In 2008, trapped gas exploded in the Foursquare Mine outside of Fessenden. Three men were killed outright, and six others were trapped and died before rescuers could reach them."

"That's why they hated us so," Lilly said, sighing as though it explained everything.

"The families of these nine men sued," Sarah continued. "They claimed the exhaust fans in the mine weren't working and that the company knew it. But Eagle brought in experts who testified a nearby lightning strike had set off methane in the mine. An act of God, Steven told the court."

"And the jury agreed," Steven said. "It's not unheard of."

"It's no more far-fetched than a woman transferring money between accounts to implicate someone else, is it?"

Steven opened his mouth to say something, but nothing came out.

"Based on Steven's testimony, the families lost their lawsuit."

"We settled out of court," Steven said.

"Point taken. When the families realized they would lose, they settled with you, but for token amounts, right? Enough to bury their dead and buy groceries for six months, but not enough to replace the earnings the men would have earned.

"And you," she said to Steven, "were slow to catch on. You knew of a Pavlos Bouras, but they kept referring to Paulie. There's a whole family of Bourases in that part of West

Virginia, so you didn't make the connection until Nora had established herself."

No one spoke for several seconds until Lilly, in a tremulous voice, asked, "What do we do now?"

Sarah raised her eyes to the ceiling and took a deep breath. She had rehearsed how to handle this moment. "You heard Ginny say, 'We deserve it. Nora... and David.'"

She paused, making certain they'd caught her emphasis. "Nora's son has autism."

During the months when she worried about Kellan's failure to speak, Sarah had studied the condition. "Not the most severe kind," she said. "He's functioning, but I gather he's at Level 2: difficulty communicating and relating to others, repetitive motion, focused on a single thing to the exclusion of everything else. He requires adult supervision and the kind of education you won't find in Fessenden, even if you can afford it."

"Is that what this is all about?" Lilly said, once again wanting to draw a curtain over the revelations.

"Not entirely. That may have been why Nora came here— why Eleanor sent her—but once she got a taste of the good life...." Nora's plaintiff words came back to her: You have no idea what it's like.

"She's cared for David for a decade," Sarah said. "when his father discovered David's problems, he abandoned her. She came here to get the money to help her son, but when she arrived, our lifestyle overwhelmed her. Remember her saying she felt as though she'd been let out of prison? She saw what an accident of birth had denied her, and she wanted it all."

Sarah turned and gave Steven her full attention. "Dad, you owe it to this family to help them. I want you to do so. You cheated them—"

"The company did this. I didn't."

"Cheated them out of their grandfather's life and his

income. They were never rich, but Paulie's death put them into a state of poverty from which they've never recovered. You must make things up to them, and you have the means to do it."

"Steven?" Lilly said.

He shook his head, but she and Lilly would work on him until he caved.

"What happens next is up to you," Sarah said. "Your relationship with Nora is your business. She can stay and live off you. You can send her home. It's all the same to me. But David is your grandson and needs the help you would provide if Kellan had this condition."

While she said that, Sarah wasn't convinced it was true. Over the past few months, she'd discovered how little she knew them.

"Victor and Kellan are my family," she said. "With them, I have everything I need."

Not quite. Sarah had lost her business and her shot at being someone other than Kellan's mother. But in the early hours of the day, as she'd recalled David's fixation with his phone, inability to communicate, and his rocking back and forth, she'd wondered whether young adults with autism couldn't find success working in a bakery. Measuring, mixing, kneading, forming dough into loaves, and feeding them into a steam oven—weren't these all repetitive tasks she could teach them? Wasn't this a business in which she could be of some use? She wouldn't know unless she tried.

"This is where I belong," she said.

James H. Lewis is the author of five previous novels, including the Chief Novak series of police procedurals. *Belonging*, a family drama, was first released on Kindle Vella. He is a former journalist, public media executive, and consultant to non-profit organizations. Lewis is a member of The Author's Guild, Pennwriters, and Pittsburgh South Writer's Group. Having lived all over the United States, he and his wife Julie now make their home in Pittsburgh where they dote on their grandchildren.